BRED IN THE GAME

Lock Down Publications and Ca$h Presents

Bred in the Game

A Novel by *S. Allen*

Lock Down Publications
P.O. Box 944
Stockbridge, Ga 30281

First Edition July 2021
Printed in the United States of America

Lock Down Publications
Like our page on Facebook: Lock Down Publications @
www.facebook.com/lockdownpublications.ldp
Book interior design by: **Shawn Walker**
Edited by: **Lashonda Johnson**

Stay Connected with Us!

Text **LOCKDOWN** to 22828 to stay up-to-date with new releases, sneak peaks, contests and more…
Thank you!

Submission Guideline.

Submit the first three chapters of your completed manuscript to ldpsubmissions@gmail.com, subject line: Your book's title. The manuscript must be in a .doc file and sent as an attachment. Document should be in Times New Roman, double spaced and in size 12 font. Also, provide your synopsis and full contact information. If sending multiple submissions, they must each be in a separate email.

Have a story but no way to send it electronically? You can still submit to LDP/Ca$h Presents. Send in the first three chapters, written or typed, of your completed manuscript to:

LDP: Submissions Dept
P.O. Box 944
Stockbridge, Ga 30281

DO NOT send original manuscript. Must be a duplicate.

Provide your synopsis and a cover letter containing your full contact information.

Thanks for considering LDP and Ca$h Presents.

Dedication

This book is dedicated to all the men and women who continue to strive tirelessly in our struggle to achieve Growth and Development, and without regret continue to stand on Nation Business.

Acknowledgment

Shout out to CEO Cash and the rest of my LDP family. Lock Down Publications is a brand and I appreciate the opportunity to be part of it. I'm going to continue to stand on this business with an iron fist! To all my haters, you know I have to show y'all some love because without y'all and y'all energy this wouldn't be possible. Just know, I'm on the beach with a bottle of Cîroc laughing at you simple-minded under-achievers— laughing all the way to the bank. Remember Men do what they want, boys only do what they can.

Chapter 1

"Rocks, blows, weed, park!" I yelled as I stood on the corner of 51st and Woods.

My hand rested in the pockets of my Marc Jacobs coat, its hood shielded me from the blistering Chicago wind. It was the middle of February and it was cold as shit out here. It was just another night in the concrete jungle of Englewood, amongst the savages trying to get to the money. It was 9:30 p.m., fifteen minutes before we shut down the block, and I had only made twenty-five hundred dollars which was kibbles and bits when you're used to making no less than five gees a night. On 51st and Woods you could get any drug your heart desired, from crack cocaine, heroin, ex-pills to exotic marijuana.

I chose to hustle the heroin because of the consistent clientele and money flow. Dope fiends are different from my other drug addicts. Unlike crackheads, heroin is a physical high, and crack cocaine is mental. You can go a day without smoking crack, but you couldn't miss a day shooting up that defense. Unless you were trying to get extremely sick.

The area I hustled in on 51st was governed by the GDs, Gangsta Disciples. I was a lieutenant for the gang and have been since I was fifteen years old. In a city plagued with murder and mayhem, the gang culture was epic and many goons chose to be a part of the culture, thus making me choose a side. I chose the Disciples. Hearing tires crushing through the snow behind me caused me to look back on alert. My hands, now resting on the handle of my Glock .40. Our dope-line was making a lot of money over here.
The stick-up boys and rivals were always lurking. So, we had to be on point. Seeing the black Tahoe creeping up the block my nerves became at ease. Seeing it was one of the guy's whip, named Vic. The SUV came to a stop, as the passenger side window came down.

"Aye, Lil Tony! Let me holla at you real quick," I heard my man's say from inside the whip.

"What's good, G?" I greeted, now at the passenger's window. The smell of potent sour diesel he was smoking on smacked me in the face.

"I need to holla at you about some business. What time y'all shutting the block down?" Vic inquired, as he took a pull from the blunt, exhaling the smoke through his nose.

"We about to shut down, right now," I responded, as I saw the security shuffling the last dope-fiends off the block.

"Shop closed! Shop closed!" I yelled to the workers enforcing my authority, lettin' 'em know to shut it down.

"Come take a ride with me, Lil Tony," Vic said.

Five minutes later, I was in the passenger seat of Vic's Tahoe pulling on the blunt he passed me.

"So, what's up, G? What you wanna holla at me about?" I probed, while I hit the blunt. The strong THC evading my lungs putting me in a hazy state.

"Listen, my nigga, this is for your ears and your ears only. You know the chico who Big Bam was getting his work from? The shit that had—"

"That had everybody on the Westside overdosing?" I said, finishing Vic's sentence.

"Yeah, exactly! You know Big Bam only stopped fucking with him because he started giving him the bricks for fifty gees. Then he saw how fast niggas was running through that shit. His greedy ass upped the ticket to eighty a key."

"So, what that got to do with us? Big Bam doing life plus thirty in the feds, he's been out the picture," I said, trying to get Vic to the point.

"Let me finish, shorty. When Big Bam stopped fucking with dude he found another plug. The chico got in his feelings because he was losing out on that paper and put the feds on Big Bam. Bam sent the paperwork out, it's official the chico is a cold rat."

"So, what are you saying, fam?"

"What I'm saying is the chico is free rec and I know where he lays his head at."

I glanced over as Vic made a left on State Street. A sinister smirk was plastered on his face. With venom dripping off his tone, he says, "Down for a lick?"

I thought about how. In fact, the chico was holding onto some major paper and supplying the city with his fentanyl cut heroin, that was closing caskets in the city. I started envisioning riding around the city in foreign whips, as clear diamonds hung from my neck. My time of being a block nigga would be exiled. Without knowing, my hand clutched the rubber grip of my hammer that fitted snugly on my waistline, as a chill went through my entire body from the thoughts of balling. Vic passed me the blunt and I took a strong pull.

"Let's do this, my nigga," I said, as weed smoke escaped my nostrils.

"That's what I'm talking about, Lil Tony. Let's get active," was Vic's only reply, before he hit the ATT button on the 15-inch Sony deck.

The four twelves in the back of the truck banged a track from *Only the Family,* shaking the concrete. We rode around the city plotting and scheming into the wee hours of the morning. Plotting our rise to power and the chico's deadly demise.

Chapter 2

A Week Later

It was 11:30 at night. Vic and I sat behind the tint of a Crown Victoria dressed in all black. A mini-Draco assault pistol rested on my lap. The 100-round drum attached to the weapon made it look futuristic like some shit off the Transformers. The anticipation of the robbery had my stomach in a knot. I had committed robbery before, but this was different. The chico was connected to The Cartel, so he wasn't just anybody. If our identities were ever found out, it could very well cost us our lives.

I was always taught that proper preparation prevents poor performance. With that being said, the chico would have to go. Period! Being in the streets so long I learned that humans are creatures of habit, and the chico had one hell of a habit-a pussy habit. Through strategic surveillance, we found out the chico was cheating with a neighborhood chick named Maria. Every night he would sneak off and come home at about 12:15. Vic and I sat in complete silence, our minds engulfed in getting this money.

"This muthafucka ain't coming, G," I said, breaking the silence. I looked at my iPhone and the time read, 1:30 a.m. I was starting to become restless.

"Just chill, Lil Tony. Have patience, the nigga gotta come in the crib," Vic retorted.

"Yeah, I hope so," I replied, just as we saw a black Escalade pull into the driveway of the house we were stalking.

"Showtime, playboy!" Vic said excitedly and pulled his ski mask over his face.

I followed suit, putting my Jason hockey mask over my face, hoodie over my head, and pulling the drawstrings on my hoodie. Identity now concealed. We watched as the chico got out of the truck and staggered to the front door. He was apparently tipsy. As if on cue, we slid out of the Crown Victoria and crept up on the chico. He never heard us coming. I put the Draco to the back of his head. The chico felt the cold barrel against his melon and reached for his waist where his .38 snub nose rested.

Whop!

I swung the baby choppa connecting it with the chico's skull, it split on impact. Pulling the slide back, I put a 7.62 round in the deadly chamber.

"We're here for the money and dope. This a robbery my nigga, don't make it a homicide," I sneered from behind my mask, meaning every word.

His warm blood dripped to the snow from his open head wound. I relieved him of the loaded .38 that was on his waist.

"Okay, migo, take the drugs! I have ten gees, please my wife and daughter are here! Please don't hurt them," the chico pleaded.

Vic snatched his 5'9, 130-pound frame up. "Open the door, nigga," Vic growled putting the Glock .40 under his chin.

The chico fumbled with the keys until he found the right one. After putting the key in the lock mechanism, he turned it and the door opened. Vic forcefully pushed him inside the house causing him to land on his face. We entered the home, guns drawn and extended, ready for any sudden surprises. Closing the door behind him and locking it, I found the light switch and flicked it on. The light invaded the room.

The chico's home was immaculate. The black sectional sofa took up most of the living room along with the large television that hung on the wall. Pictures of family and friends plastered the wall as well. The Peruvian rug on the hardwood floor that seemed to have cost some gees, was now stained with the chico's blood that leaked profusely from the gush, caused by the Draco.

"Now, I'm gonna ask you one time. Where is the money and the drugs?" Vic asked, with sinister intent.

The chico wiped blood out of his eyes. "I—have a—safe upstairs! Please don't hurt my family!"

Vic grabbed the chico by the collar and headed up the spiral staircase to his bedroom, with me following behind them. If the chico tried any bullshit, I was surely going to down his ass without blinking. We stopped at a door in the middle of the upstairs hallway and the chico pushed the door open.

"Roberto, is that you?" I heard a woman's voice say from inside the confines of the dark master bedroom.

The chico flicked on the bedroom light.

"Aaahhhh!" the woman screamed at the sight of her husband's bloody face and two masked men clutching firearms.

"Shut up, bitch, before we pop your ass," Vic threatened, grabbing the woman by her long hair and dragging her from the bed onto the floor. Her naked breasts flung wildly as she was forced to the floor in just her panties.

"Please don't hurt my wife! The safe is in the closet," the chico informed us over his wife's sobs and pleas.

I snatched him up violently and walked him over to the walk-in closet. A large floor safe resided in the corner of the closet with a digital padlock securing its contents.

"Open it," I commanded with aggression, pushing the Draco to the center of his back. After he pushed in some numbers the safe remained closed. "Open the fucking safe, nigga," I sneered. I was getting more impatient by the minute.

My attention was momentarily diverted when I heard Vic say, "Shut up, bitch!"

Then I heard a slap. I couldn't see what was going on from inside the closet, but I knew it couldn't be good. My focus was on the chico and getting this money. The chico pushed some numbers in again and on the second attempt, the green light on the digital padlock appeared. The safe was now open. What I saw in the safe made me freeze like a deer caught in the headlights. Staring me in my face was 15 kilos of heroin and rows upon rows of dead presidents. If only the world could have seen my facial expression from behind my mask. I probably could have been a representative for Colgate.

"Now please take it and go," the chico cried, bringing me out of my trance.

Quickly scanning the closet, I found a large Gucci luggage bag and forcefully snatched it, and began filling it with the safe's contents. After emptying the safe, I ushered the chico out of the closet with the chopper to the back of his medulla.

When we walked out of the closet, I couldn't believe the sight before me. Vic's bare ass cheeks were fully exposed, his camouflage cargo pants were to his ankles, and he was balls deep, pumping in and out of the chico's wife. Her pleas for help were muffled, due to the pillow Vic had used to smother her face, while he forcefully raped her. This was not part of the plan and rape was something I did not condone. I rushed over and pushed Vic off the woman.

"What the fuck you doing, nigga?"

"What the fuck you mean what I'm doing? Having a lil fun. Why you tripping? You should get you some of that shit," Vic had the nerve to say, as he pulled up his pants almost out of breath.

The woman leaped from the floor in tears and into the arms of her husband. To say I was heated would be an understatement. Vic had taken off his ski mask exposing his identity, which meant the robbery could only end one way. I looked at Vic in pure disappointment, while he was buckling his belt, smiling like a sick maniac. My M.O. wasn't women and kids, and the stupidity of his actions left me with only one choice.

"Please, amigo, you have what you came for! Now please leave us be," the chico pleaded.

I raised the Draco, pointing it at his face.

"Noooo!" he screamed.

I squeezed the trigger.

Cha! Kah!

The Draco spit a 7.62 round that found its home in the chico's head. The special Glaser round danced around his skull turning his brain into mush before it exited the back of his head staining his wife's face with the warm, gooey, copper-smelling brain tissue. The hot shell casing ejected from the powerful Draco littered the plush carpet. The chico's soul traveled to the afterlife before his body had even fallen to the floor. He felt nothing but the white sharp pain, then darkness. His wife knelt beside him after witnessing his execution, holding his head in her lap with a quarter of it missing.

She mumbled something in Spanish, then she looked up at me with fire in her tear-stained eyes, she sneered, "Puta."

Boc! Boc! was the sound from Vic's Glock .40 as he shot the woman twice in the head. Thus, giving her the same deadly fate as her husband.

I jumped from the thunderous reports of the .40 and turned to see Vic holding the smoking gun. I said, "Let's get up out of here."

When we turned to leave, to our surprise a little girl holding a teddy bear stood in the doorway. A look of fear and confusion apparent on her young face. Me and Vic froze. Seeing the gruesome scene before her, the little girl who could be no older than seven years old let a tear escape her eye.

"We gone, G," I said, and rushed past the little girl with the Draco and Gucci bag.

Taking the steps three at a time, I exited the front door but stopped in mid-stride when I heard a single gunshot. It didn't take a rocket scientist to figure out what had just transpired. Vic came running down the stairs looking like a crazed lunatic. We hopped in the Crown Victoria and pulled off into the night of the grimy streets of Chicago, adding a triple homicide to the already high murder rate.

"Fuck—a little girl, my nigga. What the fuck is wrong with you?" I hissed at Vic as he drove down the Dan Ryan expressway.

The rape was one thing, but to murder an innocent child was a whole other demonstration. I was furious. And my blood began to boil.

"What you tripping for, Tony? What was I supposed to do? Let her live so she can grow up and avenge her parents' deaths, or worse, identify us to the pigs? Stop acting all scared and shit! We're about to get to a bag, my nigga!" He said, smiling from ear to ear like he had it all figured out.

My mind began to wonder about the money and the drugs in the backseat. I was brought up in the streets by an old head by the name of Pop's Johnson. He always preached to me that in order to be a gangsta, you first had to become a man. Manhood is based on your morals and principles. One of my principles was women and kids were off-limits, and tonight I was going to stand on that plan. I quickly formulated a plan.

"Drop me off on 39th and Prairie at my Uncle Clyde's crib," I said staring out the window.

"I thought we were going back to the hood to split the take?" Vic questioned.

"We can do it at Clyde's crib. What's the sense of going all the way to 51st, when you're gonna have to drop me off anyway?"

"Whatever, fam," Vic replied, then turned up the music.

Ten minutes later we were pulling up in the parking lot of the Ida B. Wells housing projects. I called it the zone. My Uncle Clyde and my cousin K-T resided in these same projects.

"Pull up in the back of this building," I said, pointing to where I wanted Vic to go, while at the same time scanning the area to see if anybody was outside. I saw nobody.

Vic pulled behind the building and killed the engine. This would be my only chance and opportunity. As Vic reached for the bag in the backseat, I reached for the Draco that laid under my seat-that was now on my lap.

"You know that lil' girl could've grown up to be somebody? Now, she will never get to experience womanhood, have children, get married or grow to flourish into something great."

Vic looked over at me, then to the Draco that was on my lap, pointed in his direction. He let out a slight chuckle. "Nigga, you watching too much of that Dr. Phill shit. Let's go up in here and split this shit up so I can leave you and your feelings," he said sarcastically, which angered me even more.

He thought this shit was a game. Without blinking, I squeezed the trigger, the recoil from the choppa made the gun slightly jerk in my hand. The hot slug hit Vic in the side, knocking him out and severing some of his intestines. He went into shock as he grabbed his side. He felt the burning sensation from the 7.62 while the warm fresh blood seeped through his fingers from the destruction the round caused. Now he knew shit was real.

"Bitch ass—nigga—you just shot—me? We got—enough shit—to never—look back—you taking shit—personal?" Vic said, with blood coming out of his mouth.

I thought about the innocent face of the young girl. A tear escaped my eye, just as Vic made a weak attempt for the Glock on his waist. I squeezed three rapid sessions, hitting his head, neck, chest, and blowing his brains on the driver's side window. I snatched the Gucci bag off his lap and hopped out the whip, leaving gun-smoke, shell cases, and a dead body.

****

"Damn cuz, that's a lot of shit," My cousin said as we stared at the neatly wrapped kilos and the money that laid on the floor at our feet.

My cousin K.T. was only eighteen years old, but he was ahead of his time when it came to the street shit. He was also affiliated with the Gangster Disciples and we were close as thieves.

"Listen, K.T., you can't let nobody know about this shit, you hear me?" I warned in a serious tone, making sure he understood me correctly.

After we counted the money, I was pleased to see my bag with a lil' over a hunnid thousand which was more than I had seen in my twenty-three years of life at one time. First thing I was gon' do was get in contact with some niggas I knew, who had a lil' money, and let them know I had that Dino on deck. I was gon' take the fifteen bricks to the table and shake a bomb and more than triple the fifteen keys, I was about to flood the streets I thought to myself. Then, I was going to invest in some artillery, FNs and Dracos. The streets were going to be in my grasp and I was going to make K.T. enforcer. My thoughts of financial success were interrupted when we heard my Uncle Clyde coming up the stairs.

"Hurry up! Help me hide this shit," I said.

Me and K.T. put the work and money back in the Gucci bag and hid it in the closet just as Uncle Clyde walked into the bedroom.

"Junior, who you in here talking to?" He asked K.T.

"What's up, Uncle Clyde?" I said greeting my Uncle.

"Hey, Lil' Tony, didn't even know you were over here. I just came into the house. Police are every damn where. They just found some nigga sitting in the car all shot up and shit."

K.T. looked at me.

"Y'all make sure y'all stay in this house until that shit clears up out there."

"You got that, Uncle Clyde," was my only reply.

There was no witnesses and I knew I would get away with this body. Now it was time to get to this money, or so I thought.

Chapter 3

"On today's top story police have released the names in a violent triple homicide that happened on the city's Southside. Let's go to Vanessa Johnson who is live at the scene on 71st and Peoria, where the brutal murders took place. Vanessa can you tell us what is going on..."

I sat up from doing my last set of sit-ups, grabbed the remote, and turned up the volume on the television. Hearing about the murders caught my attention. I was restless ever since I caught the bodies, and unable to sleep, as my dreams haunted me. Seeing the little girls' face over and over in my head made me have a nervous feeling and the only way to keep the bloodshed out of my head was to exercise. I focused my attention back on the news and listened intensively.

"Thank you, Carol, what seems to have been a home invasion has turned deadly. Police say the home behind me was owned by Roberto Garcia, a known drug dealer who has served time in federal prison. Mr. Garcia was 53-years of age. Also found in the home deceased was his wife Amanda Garcia as well as their 6-year-old daughter, Heaven Garcia; all found unresponsive at the crime scene. Investigators at the scene found an empty safe in Garcia's bedroom and believe the motive for the crime was a robbery. Police would like anybody with information on this horrific crime to please notify the Chicago Police Department." "Thank you, Vanessa, on other news—"

I turned off the TV and went to the bathroom to throw up in the toilet. Seeing that lil' girls' face on the news made me sick to my stomach. Looking at my reflection in the mirror, a monster stared back at me. My eyes were bloodshot from countless hours of being awake. My shoulder-length dreadlocks were unmanaged, looking like a wild lion's mane on my head. The tattoo over my eye read *Relentless*. It gave me the look of a hardened criminal fresh from out of the penitentiary, even though I had never been. My life was moving at a fast pace. I was really starting to question if what I was doing in the streets was really worth it. After showering, I got dressed in stonewashed Rock Revival denim jeans, a red Champion hoodie, and a fresh pair of Nike boots. Putting on my Pelle Pelle leather jacket, I left the crib. My destination...the car lot to cop me a whip.

The African salesman looked at me crazy at the Dodge Car lot up north, when I laid 10 bands on his office table for the money down, on a new 2019 Dodge Durango SRT that was on the showroom floor. It was matte black with a peanut butter interior. I had to have it! After he accepted the blood money, he did the paperwork and issued me some temporary tags. An hour later I was pulling off the lot in my new whip. The new leather smell from the interior invaded my nose.

I immediately used my iPhone and Bluetooth to activate my playlist. The music from my phone now playing from the custom speakers inside the truck. *Calboy* and *MoneyBagg Yo's* song *Unjudge Me* pounded inside the Durango. Next, I was going to go get fleet. I had been trapping hard and stacking money and neglected to buy the latest fashions. It wasn't a priority at the time, getting money was.

"Good morning, sir. How can I assist you?" A cute ass, Puerta Rican brickhouse asked. As I entered the Gucci store downtown Chicago. Her name tag said, *Marcy*. Shorty was thick as fuck!

"What's up, baby girl. I'm trying to get myself together," I said, licking my lips. This was a bad bitch.

"Right this way, sir," she said, with a seductive look of her own and lead me to where the Gucci jeans were. I tried on a few fits, got myself together, and made my way to the counter for my merch.

"That will be sixty-eight hundred dollars," Marcy said, sounding sexy as hell.

I pulled out a ridiculous amount of blue faces and counted out the bread. After paying for my shit, she gave me my change. I asked for her number and she was more than willing to let me have it. I stored the number in my phone and left. It was funny when a nigga was struggling, he was struggling, but when that bag was all the way up, it seemed like the world was in your palms.

****

It had been two weeks since I hit the lick on the chico and things had dramatically changed on my block. Dope fiends stood in a single file line waiting to get served the best dope on the Southside, my dope. The bricks I robbed the chico for was cut with fentanyl, this I found out after about three fiends dropped dead. The shit was too strong. So, I was able to cut the dope tremendously, turning the fifteen keys into twenty-one with ease and it was still potent. Having a major influence with the guys helped my vision and plan manifest without question. I hit Pops with five bricks off the muscle since he controlled our area, in return he gave me full reign over the hood.

Thus, letting me off the leash to do as I pleased with the drug traffic in the area. I called a mandatory meeting with foe-nem and G-packs. One thousand dollars worth of dope would be passed out to the workers on the block. Eighty percent of all the profits off G-packs would be returned to me, with the workers keeping 20%. The average worker went through at least twenty packs a day so everybody was eating. The security on the block was solid. Using some of the paper, I invested in some artillery, Draco's, FNs, Ars, and a few Glocks. I had enough firepower to arm fifty men, I was playing no games!

The heat had died down from the murders but a few of the guys were starting to ask about Vic and his whereabouts. It had been two weeks since I bust his head. At first, I started to feel a tinge of guilt, but then swallowed that pill and chalked his death up to his lack of integrity and dignity. The game was cold, but it was fair. The money was coming in hand over fist and my worries had surpassed until she called my phone.

Me and K.T. were in my Durango smoking on some Gorilla Glue, politicking about expanding our drug dealing to Bloomington, Illinois when my phone vibrated on the clip of my Gucci belt.

"Hello," I answered.

"Lil' Tony…oh my God they killed him! They killed him," Tamika, Vic's baby mama, cried into the phone.

"Slow down, shorty. Who killed him?" I asked faking ignorance.

"I don't know but he's dead."

"Calm down, Tamika, I'm on my way," I said as if I was shocked by Vic's murder.

This shit was crazy! I handled that work almost three weeks ago and all of a sudden, she calls me crying and shit. I had to play the role of a supportive homie so I could go holla at shorty.

"Fam, let me drop you off real quick. I got to handle something real fast," I told K.T.

After dropping him off at Uncle Clyde's crib. I made my way to the Westside of the city. Vic and Tamika lived on Chicago Avenue and Springfield, the stronghold for the Vicelords, an opposition to us GDs, so my FN was definitely rested under the seat. It was 10:00 at night when I turned on the block of Springfield. The block was remotely quiet as I parked behind a blue minivan. Pulling my cellphone out I attempted to call Tamika's phone to let her know I was downstairs, but her phone went straight to voicemail.

Fuck this hoe ain't answering for? I thought.

I got out the whip and when I did, I heard, "*Freeze! Put your fucking hands where I can see 'em.*"

After scanning the perimeter, I was shocked to see police officers running through gangways and pointing their pistols. Unmarked Crown Victoria cars with red and blue lights came to a screeching halt and doors flung open.

"Freeze muthafucka!" I was boxed in, nowhere to run.

What was this? I thought but would soon find out.

A big Fazion Love-looking dude rushed me. Turning me around, he slapped cold cuffs around my wrist.

"Anthony Banks, you are under arrest. Anything you say can and will be held against you in a court of law. You have the right to an attorney and all the rest of that bullshit."

I couldn't believe this shit. My nerves were shook as I watched them pull the FN from under the seat. Once I was put in the squad car, I knew it was gonna be a minute before I saw the streets again.

Chapter 4

Cook County Jail

After getting processed into the Cook County Jail on 26th and California, I was housed on Division 6 for young, violent offenders who were to get a boatload of time. I had four counts of 1st Degree Homicide, one count of home invasion, and possessing a firearm by a felon. I hadn't even made it to my preliminary hearing and they were already talking about the death penalty. Come to find out, Vic told his baby mama about the robbery we were going to perform on the chico. When Vic was found murdered, Tamika sent them in my direction. Now they had a face to the case and if that ain't fucked up enough, my fingerprints were found on the doorknob inside the home, placing my body at the scene. I was in a fucked-up predicament. Since Tamika gave the people the details of the homicide it would be hard to fight.

When I walked in Division 6 with my bedroll slung over my right shoulder, I got a few mean mugs and cold stares. I was assigned to the lower tier to a cell that was in the corner of the dayroom. Pulling up my sagging pants I made my way to my cell. When I entered, an older cat sat at the small desk rolling up a jailhouse cigarette. He stood up and looked me up and down as I put my belongings on the empty top bunk.

"What's up, youngblood, where you from?" he asked lighting the cigarette with a match.

"I'm from fifty-first and Woods," I answered.

"You ever been in the county before?" he asked with a stone facial expression.

"Naw," I replied dryly.

"Well, welcome to Gladiator school, shorty. My name's Slick from the Westside, Black Soul Nation."

This was my first time in jail, but my big homie Pops had always told me jail stories about Cook County and Statesville

Penitentiary. He always told me that one day I would see the county and he prepared me for it.

The old man, my cellie, had just gang banged on me, so I had to represent and let my affiliation be known.

"GD—Fifty-first and Woods, Murda Block," I said and made the sign of a pitchfork with my hand representing my nation.

The old man was about to respond until four dudes came to my cell.

"What's good, fam, you GD?" A dude with long braids asked before he stepped inside the confines of the small cell.

"Yeah, I'm from Murda Block." Letting him know I was plugged in.

"That's what's up. My name's Jilla, I'm from Robert Taylors, Vulture City. We got word you were on your way. Grab your shit, G. We got a cell for you," Jilla said.

I grabbed my bedroll off the top bunk and made my way out of the cell. The old cat, Slick, gave me a mean mug as I left. I knew at that time the old nigga might be a problem so I would make it my business to stay out of his lane.

"Here, G." One of the guys that went by the name of Capone handed me a pillowcase full of items. Soup, toothpaste, toothbrush, shower shoes, deodorant, and a small plastic baggie with some tobacco in it. It was a jailhouse care package.

"Gratitude," I said accepting the bag.

"What you locked up for, G?" Jilla asked, once we got to the cell I would reside in while I fought my case.

"I'm locked up for some homicides," I replied.

Jilla tilted his head to the side like he was pondering something heavy on his mind. "Wait a minute, you cased up for the robbery shit with the Mexican?" Jilla probed.

"Yeah, that's the case I'm on," I said, watching as Jilla's demeanor changed.

"You bitch ass nigga. You murked that lil girl, huh?" Jilla said, through clenched teeth before he swung and punched me in my eye.

The impact from the blow caused me to see a bright light, then I saw another. The GDs proceeded to punish me in the cell with punches to the head and face and kicks to the ribs. I could smell what seemed to be copper on the warm liquid that leaked from the wounds on my head and face. The GDs beat me unconscious.

"Bitch as nigga we don't kill no kids," was all I heard, before I slipped into complete darkness.

When I awoke from my small coma, I was handcuffed to a hospital bed in Cermak, the jail hospital. I suffered a fractured jaw, two broken ribs, and a dislocated shoulder blade. Word around the county was the GDs violated me for shooting and killing a lil girl, something I didn't do. The GDs was like a business with a corporate structure. We had rules we had to abide by and one of those rules was to never hurt women or children, which I was charged with. So, my violation was carried out.

These niggas didn't even hear my side of the story, they just crushed me. The thought of it all had me perplexed. My injuries and predicament didn't stop those crackers from seeing me for my court date though. I was put in a wheelchair and taken to a room where there was a small monitor on a large oak desk. My preliminary hearing would be held on this monitor. Armed Correctional officers stood on both sides of me like I was in any condition to buck authority.

The whole process was to see if it was enough evidence to bond me for trial. The District Attorney was some slew-footed, penguin body, cat-licker, who made me out to be the monster that I wasn't.

"Your Honor, in the case of Anthony Banks, the state of Illinois wants to proceed to bond Mr. Banks over for trial."

"On what grounds?" the Judge asked, adjusting his wire-framed glasses on his long pelican nose.

"On the grounds of physical evidence. Your Honor, Mr. Banks' fingerprints were found at the scene of the crime where the Garcia family was executed in cold blood. We also have a witness that is going to testify that her boyfriend, Victor Brown informed her that he and the defendant planned to evade the home of the Garcia's in search of money and drugs, the same home Mr. Banks' fingerprints were found."

"Do we have Mr. Brown in custody as well?" the judge asked.

The District Attorney took a sip from her Styrofoam cup of water before she continued, "No, your Honor. Mr. Brown was found shot to death in his car on the Southside. After investigations, Homicide Investigators also found Mr. Banks' fingerprints as well as his DNA on a cigar, containing marijuana inside the vehicle. Mr. Banks is also charged in that homicide."

I put my head down. The shit was getting worse and worse by the minute. The more the DA talked, the more I saw my future becoming further and further away from reality.

"Your Honor, the state of Illinois recommends Mr. Banks be held without bond. He has serious gang ties to the Gangster Disciples and has a negative influence over these individuals and is also a flight risk. Thank you." The DA sat down with a look of confidence that made the hair on my neck stand up.

I tried to mentally find a way out of this nightmare, but I was coming up short. The judge cleared his throat, he stared down at me before he spoke, "Mr. Banks, I totally agree with the District Attorney. You have been charged with some heinous crimes and the City of Chicago needs to be protected from men like you. You have been involved with drugs, violence, and gang activity. A six-year-old girl was murdered in cold blood. I, myself, am disturbed at these acts of pure violence. You also have a Federal Detainer from the United States Government for weapons violations. You will be held without bond until your next court appearance that is set for February eleventh, the court is adjourned." The judge slammed the gavel, and it was over.

No bond, but, what made me shit bricks was the mention of the Feds.

Chapter 5

Three Months Later

Yeah, it took me that long to heal up. I was released back to Division 6. The Captain of the jail asked me did I want to go to P.C., Protective Custody, I refused. Whatever I had to face I would face as a man. I wasn't bogus. These niggas didn't even hear my side of the story. The nigga that is bogus is the reason I'm in jail in the first place. I did what I had to do as a man and as a gangsta. When I walked into Division 6, it was so quiet you could have heard a mouse fart. I spotted the old cat Slick, standing on the tier, posted with a few dudes I didn't know. Jilla noticed me walk into the unit, then walked off fast looking like he was going to get somebody or something. I continued walking to my assigned cell. When I walked into the cell it was empty. I put my belongings on the filthy mattress, on the bottom bunk, when all of a sudden, my cell door flung open.

"Yeah, nigga, you think shit sweet, huh? Now you gon' leave this bitch for real," Jilla sneered, holding a jailhouse shank longer than a high school hallway.

Two GDs stood behind him with similar tools of death. I had to do something quick. I wasn't armed so fighting wasn't an option. I would surely be killed.

"Fam, I didn't kill that lil girl. One of the bodies I'm fighting is the nigga that did. I'm GD and I stand on GD laws and policies," I said putting it on the Nation, telling the truth.

Jilla studied me for a second before he said, "Well, nigga, you got some explaining to do."

I proceeded to tell Jilla what I was charged with, without giving too much information that could haunt me later. The fact of the matter was, I didn't trust him. How could I? Them niggas just tried to end me, but I had to let it be known to the guys that I wasn't a child killer.

****

A month later I was indicted on federal weapons charges, under federal statute 922G for the FNH hand pistol that got caught up in the Durango. I called the big homie Pops and told him I needed a lawyer. He said he would Aid and Assist me in the endeavor. I had plenty of work on the streets and a good stash put up. Only K.T. knew the whereabouts and the workings of my growing empire. I called my Uncle Clyde's crib, he answered on the third ring.

You have a collect call, from Lil Tony. To accept this call press five, to block this call press 7—"

My uncle pressed five to accept the call, "Hello, Tony?" Clyde answered.

"Yeah, it's me, Unc. Listen, I don't have enough time to explain but these people got me on some bogus charges. I should be out in a minute after I prove myself innocent," I told him downplaying my situation.

"Well, is there anything I can do for you, nephew?"

"Naw, everything is all well. Unc, is K.T. around?" I asked.

"Hold on a minute, nephew." I heard my uncle call out K.T.'s name.

My Uncle Clyde and my cousin K.T. was the only family I had. Them and the GDs. Clyde took responsibility for raising me when my mom died of AIDS and my father got sentenced to seventy-five years for bank robbery and murder. I was totally a product of my environment.

"What's good, folks?" K.T. greeted the receiver.

"Listen, fam, shit got real in the field. I need you to listen and listen good. What I got in the streets needs to be collected. The rest of the legos, I'ma need you to grab them. Remember the plan we discussed about Bloomington?"

"Yeah," my cousin replied.

"Well, go ahead with that demonstration. You're a reflection of me so conduct yourself in that manner," I schooled him.

I knew I was putting a lot on K.T.'s plate, but K.T. had been around long enough. I stayed lacing him up with game. He was from my bloodline and I knew he was trained to go and wouldn't hesitate to get a nigga's chest wet about that money. I was confident in him without a doubt. It was plenty of money in Bloomington. What we were making off the dope in Chicago we could quadruple in Bloomington. Plus, K.T. was fucking a lil white chick down there. I think her name was Tiff or some shit like that. So, he knew the layout of the city, which would make his invasion that much sweeter.

After I gave K.T. the greenlight to expand, I hung up and made my way back to my cell. The GDs were still acting a little funny on Division 6, but on some real shit, I think they respected the move I put down. I was still in my feelings about how they stomped me out like I was one of the Ops. So, I tried my best to stay in my own lane. Even when you try to avoid confrontation, shit always seems to fall in your lap. The same old school, soul nigga, had a way of driving drunk, causing him to cross in my lane without using a turn signal.

It was 6:00 in the evening, around shower time. After grabbing my hygiene items and slipping on a pair of Reebok Classics, I grabbed my shower shoes and made my way to the shower room. Walking down the tier on my way to the shower the old nigga, Slick, bumped into me and kept on walking. No excuse me, my bad, my fault—none of that shit. First, I thought I was tripping and maybe I accidentally bumped him, until I looked back at him over my shoulder and caught him mugging me.

This nigga cruising for a bruising, I thought.

After my ten-minute shower, I made my way back to my cell. The entire time I thought about checking that old nigga and made my mind up to do so. I got dressed in some khaki pants that had D.O.C going down the pant leg in black bold letters and a clean white t-shirt. I left out of the cell to go and find Slick. I spotted him leaning on the rail talking to one of his cronies. Making my way toward him I saw Jilla posted on the wall. He acknowledged me with a head nod and a fake smile. I kept it moving like I didn't even see him.

When I approached the two Souls, I politely excused myself into their conversation. "Excuse me, old-head. Can I have a word with you real quick?" My hands clasped behind my back.

The old nigga looked me up and down like I was the scum of the earth, then said, "The name's Slick and Slick don't talk to no child killers or rapist. So, I think you need to move the fuck around before shit gets uncomfortable for you around this bitch, Joe," he hissed.

I stood in shock as the disrespectful words dispersed from his crusty lips. Slick was about 5'11, a hundred and thirty pounds soaking wet with boots on, but his eyes told a history of violence and mayhem. One thing about it, everybody in the dayroom was watching. If I let Slick get away with the blatant disrespect, my gangsta would forever be tested on Division 6. Shittt, not on my watch. His homie had the screwface like he wanted some smoke, so I punched his ass first. The blow to the bottom of his chin put him on his back.

When my fist connected, it felt like I broke my hand, as a sharp pain shot up my arm. In return, Slick reached in his pants and came up producing a sharp piece of steel. I backed away to give myself a few seconds to plan my next move. A few of the GDs that were involved in a spade game, after seeing the situation going on, got up and rushed to their cells.

"Put the knife down and see me with these hands. I'll beat your old ass, pussy!" I taunted him.

"Nah, muthafucka, I'm about to put this knife in your ass," he threatened through clenched teeth, then swung the rusty knife trying to poke me.

I dodged the attempt and bust his ass, the right hook landed perfectly on his exposed jaw.

"Yeah, shit real nigga! What's up, bitch!" I said watching Slick stumble from the blow.

Jilla, Capone, and a few more of the guys ran up the stairs holding locks that was tied to belts. Jilla swung the padlock. *Crack!* The sickening sound of the lock connecting with Slick's cranium could probably be heard throughout the jail. Slick's skull parted like Moses parted the Red Sea. I took this opportunity as a once-in-a-lifetime and rushed Slick with all that I had. He hit the floor as the knife slid down the tier. Me, Jilla, Capone, and folks gave Slick the ass whooping he was looking for. From that day forward I was looked at in a completely different light.

My time in Cook County jail passed by quickly. I instantly adapted to my environment and picked up fast on the way of jail life. My stress level was high as I thought about my situation at hand. The District Attorney was now saying my case was a death penalty case and if convicted I could be put to death by lethal injection. It was no way I could let that happen. While I was in the county, I met a nigga from Minnesota who went by the name Clip.

Clip was a shotgun Crip who had come to the Chi to drop off ten pounds of Gelato marijuana when he was pulled over by Chicago police for a traffic violation. After searching the trunk of his Jag the police found the pounds and now Clip was waiting to get bonded out on the 100,000 dollar cash bond. Me and Clip got cool on the spade table, he was a real nigga and carried himself like a player. One day we were kicking it, shooting the shit when he asked me about my case.

"Aye, Loc, how they got you charged for some bodies with no witness or murder weapon? I'm not trying to be in your business, but I fuck with you gangsta, and to me, that shit sounds beatable," Clip said.

"They got my fingerprints, my nigga. How can you deny that?" I explained.

Clip rubbed his beard and said, "Find a reason to be in the house. Just because they placed you at the scene don't prove you killed nobody. You don't have to prove you didn't do it. They have to prove you did. Just food for thought, G."

I stood pondering what Clip had just laid down to me.

"*Lock-in! Lock-in!*" The C.O. yelled over the loudspeaker.

"Alright, fam, I'm a holla at you in the a.m," I said and gave Clip a gangsta pound and headed to my cell.

Later that night, I laid on my back, hands behind my head staring at the ceiling. I was in heavy thought thinking about what Clip said and a light went off in my head. Like he said, me being in the house or in Vic's car didn't prove I did the shootings. At that time, I came up with a plan and master deceit. This is the play, I would tell them, people, I didn't deny being at the Garcia house. Roberto

Garcia was a drug dealer, and I did business with him on a few occasions. Once he had a BBQ and I was invited to the home.

That explains my fingerprints in the house. I would also tell them that Vic was my mans and I rotated hard with him in the streets. I've been in the car plenty of times. That's my people, why would I want to hurt him? They had no murder weapon and no witnesses. Fuck it! I'm shooting my shot. I presented my spill to my lawyer that Pops retained for my defense. The state offered me a plea of life in prison. Yeah, right. I laced my boots and got ready to go to trial.

Chapter 6

The day of my trial was a day I would never forget. The jurors were all white, ready, and willing to find me guilty and put the needle in my veins, so they thought.

"All rise for the honorable Judge McMan..."

I stood up and brushed some lint off my white button-up my Uncle Clyde sent me. He was also in the courtroom to show his support. K.T. was missing but I already knew he was in the streets conducting Nation Business. The judge emerged from the chambers and sat in the plush chair behind the large podium.

"You can be seated," the judge said and picked up some papers from his desk.

"What do we have here today?"

"The State of Illinois versus Anthony Banks. Case docket number 556A374, four counts of first-degree intentional homicide and one count of a home invasion while armed. He also has a federal detainer for weapon possession. The State of Illinois is here today to proceed with the trial," the court reporter stated to the Judge.

"Okay, let's start, shall we? Who do we have in the courtroom here today?" the judge asked.

The DA was the first to stand. "Mark Davis, District Attorney for the State of Illinois," the sleaze bucket said.

My lawyer then stood straightening the pants legs of his Ferragamo slacks. He said, "Attorney Carlito Giovanni, I will be representing Mr. Banks in his defense." My lawyer's diamond pinky ring shined hard as hell.

Pops had retained him for $50,000. He wanted $160,000 for the whole case. Carlito was an Italian, hotshot lawyer, a gangster lawyer to the streets.

"All right, Mr. Davis, let's hear what the state is representing in this case."

The District Attorney took to the stage to paint his picture to try to lead to my conviction. "What we have in this courtroom is a monster. When I say monster, I mean monster. A monster that murders families. A monster that takes the lives of innocent children, and you know for what?" The DA turned to face the jury before he continued, "For money and drugs."

"That's right people, money, and drugs. And the monster is Anthony Banks. Not only did he commit cold-blooded murder. He turned the gun on his own partner in crime only to end his life as well. The Illinois Department of Corrections was built for soulless men like Anthony Banks. Mr. Banks' fingerprints were found on the scenes of the crimes and we have a witness that is going to testify that Mr. Banks' crime partner confided in her about the robbery of the Garcia home prior to the crime committed."

"Let's hear from the witness you have for the state," the Judge requested.

Tamika walked up to the stand looking like the malnutrition stool pigeon that she was. After putting her hand on the bible, she testified saying Vic told her about the move we were going to put down on the chico for some heroin. I couldn't believe this nigga! Vic was pillow talking with this hoe about shit we were doing in the streets. She played the role of the grieving baby mama very well. To me, Tamika was nothing but a rat, straight up! After she did her thing on the stand, she smirked at me on her way out.

Dirty bitch! I thought.

The Judge gave my lawyer a chance to prove my innocence. He took a swig from his bottled water, then took the stage.

"Your Honor, what we have here is a case where a person is charged for something he didn't do. Mr. Banks and Mr. Garcia were business partners. Mr. Banks purchased heroin from Mr. Garcia a few times, even getting invited to a barbeque. So, yes, Mr. Banks has been to the Garcia residence. Was he there at the time of the murders? And if so, where is the proof? In the case of Victor Brown. Come on people, these guys have been close friends since the sandbox."

"They were together on the daily. Mr. Banks admits to being in that car plenty of times, but was he in the car when Mr. Brown was murdered? And if so, where is the proof? And yes, a firearm was found in Mr. Banks' car, but was it the weapon used in these crimes? No, it was not. All I ask is that the people of Illinois look at the facts of this case and not just assume because there is no evidence proving Mr. Banks committed these crimes, thank you," my lawyer said taking a seat next to me.

He had presented my case perfectly and I could tell I was in a good place by the look on the DA's face. At that moment he knew he had a weak case. Now, it was up to the jury to decide my fate.

It took four hours of deliberation for the jurors to come back with a verdict on my case.

"In the case of State of Illinois vs Anthony Banks, count one of First-degree homicide. Not guilty. Count two, First Degree Homicide. Not guilty."

A smile came across my hardened face as the verdicts continued.

"Count three, First Degree Homicide. Not guilty."

I could see the DA swimming in a pool of defeat while he looked busted and disgusted by the outcome of my charges.

"Count five, Home invasion while armed. Not guilty."

"That's right, Junior," I heard my Uncle say from behind me, showing his loyalty and support.

"You murdering son of a bitch!" A tall Hispanic yelled at me, until the bailiffs grabbed and restrained him, then escorted him by force out of the courtroom.

"Order in the court! Order in the court!" the Judge yelled as he banged his gavel in an attempt to restore order in his courtroom. After things quieted down a notch, my trial continued. I was found not guilty on all the bodies as well as the home invasion. I gasped as my future was back in my vision, until just as quick it became a blur. Even though I beat the State charges I still had to face my nightmare. The United States Government. I still had to fight the gun charge with the Feds.

****

It had been two weeks after I smashed the State charges, which created plenty of controversy in the news. I was lying on my bunk getting some much-needed rest.

Jilla came and woke me up. “Aye folks, they just called your name over the loudspeaker talking ‘bout getting ready for court.”

I wiped the crust from the corner of my eye and sat up.

“They probably said somebody else’s name,” I retorted.

I knew I was wrong when the C.O. came to the bars, “Banks, get ready for court!”

This has to be some kind of mistake, I thought and walked to the bars to holla at the female C.O.

“C.O. you must have the wrong person. I shouldn’t have my court dates yet,” I tried to explain to her with confusion stretched across my face.

“Banks, you have Federal court. So, let’s get going,” was her only reply, before she escorted me out of Division 6.

The C.O. escorted me to the first floor of the Cook County Jail, the booking area where two white males awaited me holding a pair of shackles and leg irons.

“Anthony Banks?” the short chubby one said.

“Yeah, what up?” I answered.

“We are with the US Marshalls. Please put your hands behind your back.”

I did as I was instructed and was loaded into a tinted black Yukon on my way to M.C.C, the federal holding facility downtown Chicago. On my way to the building, I stared out the window watching the streets pass me in a blur. The cold handcuffs were locked on my wrists as the shackles secured my ankles, preventing any form of me breaching security. I was in the grasp of a street nigga’s nightmare. The Feds.

After I was processed in M.C.C I was housed on a unit for guys still waiting to see the judge. Twenty-four hours later, I was in court for I.A. *Initial Appearance*. At the court date, I was indicted on federal weapons charges, a 922-G felon in possession of a firearm. When I was a teenager, I got caught with 250 grams of marijuana and was charged with possession with intent to deliver, which was a felony case. Even though I was only given two years of probation, the felony still stuck, thus preventing me from carrying a firearm.

My lawyer told me the Federal Prosecutor had a hard-on for me because I beat the bodies in the State. The United States Government wanted blood, and with my sentencing guidelines, I was facing zero to twenty years, 120 months for the gun. A few months later I was sentenced to a dime. Can you believe that? The cold-hearted peckerwood gave me the max. Whatever-ten years was better than lethal injection. I'm gonna take my ten like a real G. I was loaded on a bus and headed to my designated prison U.S.P. Lewisburg.

Chapter 7

Coming up I heard plenty of gruesome stories about Lewisburg Penitentiary. It was the Feds oldest prison. Gangstas, such as Al Capone, John Gotti, Bugsy Seagal, and Larry Hoover were all convicts of the bloody prison at one point. Lewisburg Penitentiary was the home of the goons within crime all over the United States. The prison bus pulled up to the Penitentiary in Lewisburg Pennsylvania at 3:30 p.m. on a hot Thursday afternoon. The prison looked like a deserted castle that I had seen on TV once. It definitely looked grimy. When the bus stopped, at least ten correctional officers waited with batons in their hands, ready to escort us into the gates of hell. A short, chubby C.O. boarded the bus with a clipboard in his hands.

"Now listen up, you maggots. When I call your name and number step to the front of the fucking bus," the redneck barked.

"Dennis Hill, three-six-zero-six-nine dash zero-five-six."

A young, white boy with a six-point star tattooed on his face stood up and made his way to the front of the bus.

"Antonio Parker, nine-six-zero-three-two dash zero-six-nine."

Some cat with a Mike Tyson face tattoo, got up and followed suit. Something about the Antonio nigga stood out, the nigga looked shiesty. It was all in his eyes when he glanced over at me as he passed by, making his way to the front of the bus.

I was going to make it my business to stay away from dude, straight up. The C.O. said a few more names, then I was called, "Anthony Banks, eight-eight-three-four-six dash four-two-four. Step to the front."

I got up and made my way to the front of the bus. I had to walk slow to prevent the leg irons from cutting into my exposed ankles. Once I was off the bus, I was led to a small, holding cage to be stripped down. A C.O. came to the cage and told me to strip. I discarded my clothing and passed them to the Correctional Officer, who then put them in a plastic bin.

"Hold your hands up, open your mouth, lift your sack, turn around, bend over—cough."

I did as I was told feeling humiliated as fuck.

"What sizes, boy?" the C.O. asked with a mug on his face.

"2-X top, 3-X pants, and 2-X underwear," I said in return.

The C.O. stepped off to get my clothes. I stood naked as the day I was born in a cold-ass cage, feeling like the animal they betrayed me to be.

"This shit's fucked up, huh, fam?" A dude asked me who was in the cage next to me.

I couldn't see him, due to the bricks that separated us. "Yeah, these some racist muthafuckas down here," I responded.

"Aye, what spot you just come from, Joe?" dude asked.

I could tell he was from Chicago from his accent and street slang.

"I just came from M.C.C Chicago. I'm fresh in," I told him.

"You from the crib?" he asked meaning Chicago.

"Yeah."

"Where you from out there?" He probed.

"I'm from fifty-first and Woods—Murda Block," I retorted.

"I'm from sixty-ninth and Wolcott—G.B.C. They call me Yayo, fam. What they call you?"

"My name's Lil Tony," I responded.

What piqued my interest was dude said his name was Yayo. If the nigga next to me was G.B.C Yayo then I was next to the street legend. Yayo and the G.B.C had dominated the streets of Chicago for almost twenty years. Yayo was their chief. The gang was now under Quavon's leadership. Yayo's younger brother, who had the murder rate high in the city, and them niggas were getting money undisputed. Yayo and I continued to conversate until the C.O. came back with our clothes.

Yayo told me he had been down for four years on his life sentence and had just been transferred from a Maximum-security prison in Louisiana called Pollock for stabbing another inmate. The C.O. passed me my prison uniform through the cage. I got dressed in the weird clothing I was given, then the C.O. unlocked my cage, and led me uncuffed to an area to stand in front of a camera to get my mug shot taken. Walking past the cage that was next to me, I looked in and got a visual of Yayo. It was definitely him. His face was the same face that was plastered all over the news when he got sentenced to life in the feds for drugs and murder. He gave me a head nod as I walked past.

When I finished getting my gangsta face snapped, I was taken inside an office where three officers sat at a table. One had on a white shirt. He was the captain. He had my file in front of him. He was the first to speak.

"You know why you're here, boy?" he asked sounding like the Grand Wizard of the Klu Klux Klan. I was about to respond until he continued.

"You are here to serve time. It says here you are an active Gangster Disciple?" he said, reading from my file. "Well, let me tell you something, boy. I'm the Captain of this boat and us here at Lewisburg don't tolerate all that nigger gangbanging shit. You only got ten years, so my advice is that you stay out the way and get back home to your lil nigglets, because here at Lewisburg, you ain't guaranteed to make it out. You get my drift?"

I remained silent and unfazed by the Captain's scare tactics. I was a man, and I was always taught to handle everything no matter what.

"Now, you will be assigned to D-house, also known as the dog pound, as we call it. Like I told you dip shit, my advice is for you to mind your business. We already had three killings over there and the summer just started. Find something positive to do with your time. Now take him to his cell."

The C.O. was leading me out of the Captain's office.

"And Banks," the Captain called out causing me to stop. "Don't let your name come across my desk or it's not going to end up good for you. Now get him out of here."

"Alright, Banks, this is your cell, welcome home," the C.O. said as I stood in front of a cell with my bedroll."

"Pop cell sixteen," the C.O. spoke into his walkie-talkie that was pinned to his shirt.

A moment later, the cell door opened. A short, stocky dude stood on the other side of the door. He was 5'9 with shoulder-length braids.

"Step in the cell, Banks," the C.O. said with authority.

I stepped in and put my belongings on the top bunk.

"Close cell sixteen," the C.O. said into the walkie-talkie, then the cell door closed.

"Where you from, thug?" the guy asked as I glanced around the crucially small living quarters.

"I'm from Chicago. Where you from?"

"I'm from Summerville, Tennessee. My name's Kilo, I'm Vice Lord," the dude said.

I thought, *Here we go again, niggas gangbanging on me.*

Kilo was a different type of dude. He said what he said but extended his hand in greeting.

"My name's Lil Tony. I'm GD from Chicago," I said, shaking Kilo's hand.

"Aye, your paperwork good ain't it?" Kilo asked, inquiring about my legal documents. Wanting to know if I stood strong on my case or snitched. Which let me know he had a distaste for rats just like me.

"Yeah, fam, I'm good. I'm one-thousand and my paperwork should be on the way as we speak," I informed him and started to make my bed.

I despised rodents with a passion, and it was good to know Kilo was on the same page in a sense.

"What you in for?" Kilo questioned and sat up in the bunk to give me room to get my things on order.

The cell was the size of a small closet in an efficiency apartment.

"I got caught with a banga and they gave me a dime."

"Yeah? I got ten for a pistol as well. I had eight months left on my sentence and was supposed to go home but I got ninety-two more months for crushing a lieutenant in U.S.P Victorville in California."

"Damn, ninety-two more months? You must've punished buddy?" I said shocked at the amount of time he got.

"Yeah, you already know, my nigga."

Me and Kilo sat up all night, with him giving me the rundown on what's going on around the prison. I ended up finding out Lewisburg was a fucked up prison. Most of the inmates were sent there for disciplinary reasons and Lewisburg had a Special Management Unit. They called it S.M.U. It was located on the Northside of the prison yard. Inmates assigned to the S.M.U. were the worst of the worst. Kilo was cool though, he even opened his locker to me and made me a meal which consisted of Ramen Noodles, mixed with cheese, nacho chips, and a cut-up summer sausage. The shit was gas, good as hell.

The next morning, after the C.O. popped our cells open, me and Kilo made our way to the recreation yard to meet up with some of my people who were said to be in the yard. The GDs, BDs, and Vice Lords ran together in something called a Coalition, an alliance. The feds were different than the state. I had never been to prison, but I knew up my way in State prison, the GDs and Vice Lords stayed beefing, but this nigga Kilo was cool as hell.

When we made it to the yard, Kilo took me to meet a Muslim-looking dude who was doing pull-ups on a pull-up bar.

"Aye Black Mac, this one of the folks that just got off the bus. His name's Lil Tony. Lil Tony this Black Mac," Kilo introduced us. Black Mac did three more pull-ups before getting off the pull-up bar.

"What's good, G? Black Mac, Memphis, Tennessee."

"Lil Tony, Chicago—Murda Block," I replied shaking Black Mac's hand.

"You need anything, family?" Black Mac asked without a smile.

"Naw, I'm good, fam. My celly got me situated," I told him.

"Your celly's a good nigga. I been to two spots with shorty. Aye but check—once you get your paperwork and you check out, I'ma rotate with you and if you want one, I can get you a hammer."

"A'ight," I replied looking over Black Mac's shoulder. A large group of Mexicans in the corner of the rec-yard looked to be in heavy conversation.

"What's up with dude and 'em over there?" I asked.

Black Mac turned around to see what I was talking about. "Those are the Surenos, they're a gang from Southern California. It looks like they have something going on. Let's walk over here." Black Mac walked us to the other side of the recreation yard.

I still kept my visual on the Mexicans. A short Hispanic with face tats seemed to be doing all the talking.

"Who is the short dude?" I inquired just in case I needed to know in the future.

"The one talking is their shot caller. His name's Joker. He is from California. He has been down for about twenty years."

Joker didn't look like much, but I could tell how his homies hung onto his words that he was somebody of importance. Joker walked away from the circle of Surenos with his hands clasped behind his back. Then all of a sudden two of the Mexicans grabbed another one by the arms, securing him as another one of them pulled a jailhouse knife from the confines of his waistline and started to repeatedly stab the one being held by his arms.

He was stabbed in his face, chest, and stomach. Blood squirted from the life-threatening wounds. Watching the violent assault play out in front of me caused me to freeze. I had shot niggas in the street multiple times, but seeing this kind of work was different. It was up close and personal. The guard tower, that sat high in the tall brick wall, that surrounded the prison, caught the assault taking place.

"Inmates, down on the ground! I repeat, inmates down on the ground or you will be shot!" the C.O. said in the guard tower over the loud intercom.

At the mention of getting shot, I hit the ground so fast you would have thought I was doing a one-count burpee seeing that AR-15 sticking out the window of the guard tower. C.O.s and medical staff rushed to the yard in an attempt to break up the assault. The one that did the stabbing briskly walked off and discreetly handed the bloody knife to one of his homies as the victim fell to the pavement. Now drowning in a puddle of his own blood. The C.O.s and medical staff loaded his punctured body on a stretcher and rushed him off the prison yard to get him to the nearest hospital. Come to find out the dude who was stabbed was a Norteno.

The Nortenos were not supposed to walk the yard of U.S.P Lewisburg as it was turf for the Sorenos, their archenemies in the streets of California as well the Bureau of Prisons. The Norteno had tried his hand, in which he paid for it with his life.

I hadn't been in Lewisburg twenty-four hours and already, somebody lost their life. I was going to call my lawyer in the AM to get him to speed up the process of sending my court documents, so I could be cleared by my homies. Once I did, my first priority was to take Black Mac up on his offer and get me a knife.

Chapter 8

Kilo

"Aye, Walker, you getting a celly," the C.O. said from the other side of my cell door.

I had been in the Lewisburg Penitentiary for almost five years. Yeah, that's right, while niggas in the streets faking at an all-time high, I've been in the battlefield, the belly of the beast, in the trenches with the gorillas and the wolves. I came to the Federal System as an immature knucklehead. Now, I'm a full-grown man with my heart a little colder. My main problem was my elite temper. I could go from zero to a hunnid real quick, and that's why I ended up catching ninety-two more months.

Til' this day I take the extra time like a soldier. A lot of other niggas would have passed out in court, or worse, told on a muthafucka to get his time knocked down. But, I kept it moving. Catching extra time was justified in all aspects of gangsterism. A lieutenant had put his hands on me, and I crushed him point blank period. My original indictment was something a lil' different. I got caught up on a humbug pistol case. I remembered it like it was yesterday.

It was 9:30 at night, I was at my baby mama's apartment watching water bubble up inside the Pyrex jar, that was on the Kenwood stove, under medium heat. My baby mama and my daughter were at Walmart doing some late-night shopping, so I had the crib to myself. My phone had been ringing off the hook none stop from smokers wanting some crack. So, I took this opportunity to cook up a fresh batch of the Devil's love potion. Standing in a pair of black Dickies pants, butter wheat Timberland boots, and a wife-beater. I poured two ounces of cocaine into the bubbling Pyrex.

While the cake bubbled, I weighed two ounces of Arm and Hammer baking soda and poured that into the Pyrex as well. While the cocaine was cooking, I went to the freezer and got a few ice cubes. I took the Pyrex off the stove. I could see the oil base from the cocaine floating on top of the pot. After dropping the ice cubes into the Pyrex, I got a fork and started whipping the drugs, stopping only to get my burning Newport from the ashtray to take a few pulls. The coolness and the heat from the boiling water caused a chemical reaction, thus causing the oil base from the cocaine to lock up.

The oil base now turned into a mushy substance resembling the texture of some mashed potatoes. My objective was to make the substance harder and harder. I added another ice cube and continued to whip the drugs with the fork. After a few more minutes the substance was now hard white. I dumped the crack on a newspaper to let it dry and cool off. I was a demon when it came to mixing and cooking drugs, specifically cocaine.

My Uncle Ricky taught me the game at the tender age of twelve years old and now at age twenty-three, the hood named me Kilo because of my abilities when it came to cocaine and the weight I moved. When the crack was ready and dry, I grabbed the razor blade, some baggies, my digital scale and went to work. I was the Lord of the crack game in Summerville, Tennessee. All my rocks weighed at 0.5 for fifty dollars. The work went fast. I was easily dumping off four ounces in bags daily, making no less than $2,800 off an ounce, you do the math.

Once I was done chopping and bagging, I hit the streets to get my grind on. Summerville was a small town outside of Memphis. We hustled way different than niggas in bigger cities. Instead of hustling off blocks, we had trap houses where the smokers could come to purchase drugs. I was a three-star branch elite for the Vice Lords so my name held weight within the M.O.B. Everybody knew me as my Uncle Ricky's henchman. Ricky was a five-star branch elite for the Vice Lords, as he had major influence and dictatorship.

My Uncle Ricky was paralyzed from the waist down and was confined to a wheelchair. He was shot in his back at a dice game in Memphis. Ricky was feared in Summerville and was known to bust his guns, so niggas stayed trying to get him out the way. My uncle also had that money. He had that throwback paper, not to mention he was a prolific gambler. The nigga had the coldest roll on dice I had ever seen. Uncle Ricky was like a God to the hood.

Later that night, after I finished making a few moves, I pulled up to one of my crack houses on the Westside of the city. Upon entering, the smell of high-grade marijuana slapped me in the face. My crew was playing PlayStation 5 on a large projector-style television. Bird, Stunna, and Dread were my young seeds that sold drugs for me. I had brought them into the Vice Lord Nation personally.

Bird was a hothead, always willing to put in some work. He was my hitter. Stunna was the real hustla out of the three. He moved his work faster, so more money went through his hands. If shorty stayed loyal to the game, he was going to have a prosperous future. Dread was a different story. He was a good soldier, but at times his mind wandered, so I stayed putting my foot in his ass for his fuck ups. When it was all said and done, he was my lil' nigga. All of them were Vice Lords, thus making us family.

"What up, Lord?" Stunna greeted me when I walked in.

"Ain't shit. What's the count?" I inquired, pertaining to the trap money from the six ounces of crack I dropped off a couple of nights ago.

"It's about ten gees, but Bud still owes for an ounce he came and got."

"Who the fuck said Bud was supposed to get an ounce?" I said confused.

Bud was one of my lieutenants I had overseeing my trap houses but as of lately Bud had been fucking up in a major way and I was getting tired of his mishaps. My anger began to boil thinking about how this nigga was doing way too much. I got my Galaxy Android off my Gucci belt and called the nigga. I didn't get an answer and it took ten minutes for dude to call me back.

"Hello!" I answered agitated as hell.

"What's good? You called me?"

"What's good? Nigga you came over here and got something without my permission?" I asked him, venom dripping from my tone. I could hear females laughing in the background.

"Yeah, I told shorty and them to let you know I was grabbing it. I had to take care of something real quick," the nigga had the nerve to say.

"You know the rules, you get up with me before you take something out *my* trap," I said.

I heard him chuckle before he said, "You got that big homie. I'm gonna get you that bread when I'm done doing what I'm doing." Then I heard the dial tone in my ear.

I stared at my phone not believing Bud had just tested my gangsta. My Uncle Ricky told me long ago that when your subordinates tested your authority it would be time to set an example. Not only did Bud try my authority, *He* tried my manhood and that didn't sit well with the kid. I tossed my phone on the couch and began addressing my delinquent crew.

"Check this out. That nigga Bud is in violation. When he comes back over here, I want y'all to text me ASAP and keep him here until I get here."

"What if he tries to leave before you get here?" Dread asked dumb as hell.

"You just make sure he doesn't," I sneered.

I collected my money, gave Stunna some more work, and left the trap, heated. I needed to calm my nerves, so I grabbed the half of blunt that was in my ashtray and lit it. The effects of the weed calmed me to a certain extent, but my anger wouldn't subside completely. Bud was tripping for sure. When I caught up with his ass, I was definitely going to get him together. For the next few hours, I rode around Summerville picking up money and dropping off drugs. For the past year, I had been getting my numbers up with the crack and it was all due to my hustla's ambition.

You see, I'm different from most niggas that hustle in my city. I hustle for a cause. Just recently I found out my mother, who happens to be a minister at First Baptist Church, had been diagnosed with cancer, not to mention, I have a baby mama and a little girl to take care of. So, my criminal endeavors were done to support my family. And at this level of the game, I had no room for shorts or niggas playing. I was ten toes down in the field. Taking a pull from a freshly rolled blunt, my phone vibrated on the clip on my belt.

Looking at the screen, I saw I had a text. It was from Dread, saying Bud was at the trap. My palms began to sweat as I made my way back to the hood to fuck this nigga up. When I pulled back up to the trap in my 2018 Range Rover, I was confused, to say the least, not seeing Bud's Challenger.

I know these niggas ain't call me for here for nothing, I thought hopping out of the whip.

As I entered the trap, the first thing I noticed was the blunt smell of crack cocaine that was evident in the air, as two crackheads sat on the couch with their lips glued to glass pipes. Stunna and Bird sat at the kitchen table bagging up work while Dread played the PlayStation. I closed the door and served the deadbolt.

"What's up? Why y'all text me if the nigga ain't here?" I questioned walking over to Stunna and Bird.

"The nigga Bud on his way over here. He said he had to drop some bread off in South Memphis. Then he said he was going to be on his way. That was thirty minutes ago," Stunna informed me.

Rubbing my freshly trimmed goatee, I said, "Alright, get these smokers up outta here."

After clearing the trap, we sat and waited patiently for Bud to arrive. My Glock rested comfortably in the confines of my Givenchy jeans while I rolled another blunt. Two blunts of Sour Diesel later there were three knocks at the door. Bud finally showed up. I stood behind the counter as I nodded to Dread to open the door. He walked in with a cigarette dangling from his lips, carrying a bag from Popeye's Chicken.

"What took you so long to open the fucking door?" Bud asked Dread in an aggressive tone, trying to lil' boy Dread.

Dread ignored him and put the deadbolt back on the door.

"What's good, Lord? Took you long enough," I said, in a cool calm demeanor.

"My bad, Joe, I had to drop this lil chick off in South Memphis."

"Oh, yeah? Seems like you forgot every real street nigga's motto."

"What's that?" Bud retorted, placing the bag of chicken on the counter.

I don't know what angered me more, the fact that he was my lieutenant, and I was the one that put him on, or this nigga was steady trying me. Whatever the case, I was about to handle this Nation Business.

"The motto is money over bitches. Especially, my money," I said through clenched teeth before I pulled the Glock off my waist and pointed the business in his face, making him look down the barrel. Then, I picked up the nail hammer with my other hand that laid on the counter. Instantly, his demeanor changed. "Now, which hammer you want?" I asked holding the Glock .40 in one hand and the nail hammer in the other. My goons watched intently as I stood on my gangsta.

"Hold up, Lord! I got half the money for the ounce I grabbed," he pleaded before reaching in his pocket to get the cash.

I pulled the slide on the Glock putting a hallow point up top, causing him to freeze like a popsicle.

"Nigga, did you come over here and grab a half ounce? Now, I said what hammer do you want?" My voice boomed throughout the inside of the trap house.

I could tell this nigga was scared as hell in the presence of death. Bud had a hell of a choice to make. Stuttering like a nervous prick, he said, "That-that-that-that one." Then pointed to the nail hammer in my left hand.

"Put your fucking hand on the counter," I commanded. Bud looked at the front door, I read his thoughts. "You try to run I'm gonna down your ass," I hissed, meaning every word while tightening my finger on the trigger.

Bud reluctantly placed his hand on the kitchen counter in front of me. I raised the hammer and brought it down with extreme force. Bud let out a piercing scream, sounding like a distressed teenage girl instead of a twenty-three-year-old street nigga. Hearing the sound from the bone being crushed in Bud's hand upon contact of the hammer was sick. Bud cradled his hand as pain shot through his body.

"Put your other hand on the counter!"

"Come on, Lord—please! I'm gonna get the rest of the money! Come on, fam," Bud's pleas fell on deaf ears.

Little did Bud know it was no longer about the money. It was about respect and principle, something at this moment, I was standing on. I put the Glock under his chin, the cold plastic on his flesh.

"Don't make me say it again," I threatened.

Tears from pain escaped his eye as he put his left hand on the counter. Bringing the hammer down on his hand I got the same reaction. The sound of broken bones and Bud screaming like a bitch. I politely laid the hammer down on the counter but still had the glizzy in this niggas face. My soldiers watched my work, seeing Bud's white bones sticking out through the flesh in his hands. I was making a statement in front of my crew. The statement was that I was the boss.

"Now the next time you think about taking something that don't belong to you without my consent, just know I'm gonna be the one to choose the hammer. Now get the fuck outta here and go get my money!" I told Bud, who was whimpering like a small child as his hands swelled at an alarming rate.

Bud had just learned a valuable lesson in life and that was to never bite the hand that feeds you. In the streets when you deal with your men it's supposed to be love and loyalty, but when that was neglected, complications could be brought forth to gain back that authority.

Chapter 9

Kilo

"Oooh baby, don't stop! Kilo, please don't stop! Right there! Oh, my God Kilo, you're hitting my spot! I'm—

about—to—cum!" My baby mama moaned as I penetrated her from the back.

Watching her ass cheeks jiggle from each thrust had me going through some things, but I couldn't blow my load yet, not before I punished this pussy. Me and baby mama, Tammy been together since 6th grade. Yeah, for real, shorty been rocking with a nigga forever. We have a ten-year-old daughter named, Precious. My princess, my star, and all of the above. My daughter is my everything.

My goal was as soon as I finished dumping off the last two kilos of coke and paid my Uncle Ricky back, I was going to be done with the game. A few months ago, I sat down with my daughter to have a serious talk, maybe too serious for a child her age but this was my daughter and I held nothing from her. I told her I could give her the world, but it was a possibility I could end up in jail again.

She looked at me with her soft brown eyes and she said, "Daddy, I don't want you to go to jail again."

Remembering the numerous times I had been to jail throughout her young life, not to mention my mom has cancer and I would have to be the one to look out and provide for her, it was a no-brainer. I loved my family more than I would ever love the streets. The situation with Bud had me vexed which is what brings me to this-punishing Tammy's pussy.

"That's right, take this dick." I watched as my ten-inch pole slid in and out of her tight walls, her juicy pussy lips gripping my meat as her juices coated my stomach and thighs.

Shorty had that wet for real. Grabbing her long hair, I rode her like the stallion she was, the scent of our sex filling the master bedroom. Tammy got up from her doggy-style position I had her in and knelt between my legs. Grabbing my cock with two hands, she slid me in and out the warmth of her mouth and started giving me head.

I watched as she licked, tugged, and sucked her juices off my dick. My baby mama was a savage in the sheets.

When she looked me in the eyes, I lost it. The vein in my dick swelled up. She knew what time it was and started sucking faster and faster, massaging my balls at the same time. Her hair in my grasp, I exploded in three long squirts, coating her throat with my seeds. Feeling the tension leave my stressed body, I heard a loud noise come from downstairs like my door was being kicked in. My daughter was at my mom's house for the weekend, yet, me and Tammy's safety was in danger. I immediately reached for the .45 on my dresser and chambered a round.

"Baby, what the fuck was that?" Tammy asked with a look of uncertainty written over her face.

Easing to the bedroom door, pole extended and ass naked, I heard muthafuckas yelling "ATF!", then footsteps rushing up the stairs. I had no time to react as my bedroom door was kicked in and agents swarmed the room like bees holding pistols and assault weapons.

"Let me see your hands! Drop the Weapon!" I was in a no-win situation, so I complied with the officers, dropped the .45, and held my hands up, dick swinging and all.

"Kaliel Walker, we have a warrant for your arrest for the assault of Daniel Williams."

I was handcuffed and placed in an unmarked car. Tammy was also cuffed up and put in a cruiser. After searching my residence, the pigs ended up finding two more hammers and two twin .38 snub noses. Damn, shit wasn't looking good. I was taken to Memphis County Jail, booked, and charged with three counts of possession of a firearm by a felon, which the feds picked up with the quickness. Tammy was let go, which was good, even though I knew she would be. She had nothing to do with my criminal activity.

The next morning, I was awakened by a chubby correctional officer saying that I had an attorney visit. After being handcuffed, I was taken to a room where two pale face crackers sat at a table. The officers sat me across two men who identified themselves as FBI agents.

"You want a cigarette, coffee, chips—anything we can get you, Mr. Walker?"

"Naw, I'm good. What y'all call me down here for?" I asked the goofy-ass agents. The agent lit a Marlboro and inhaled the cancer stick before he spoke.

"Seems like you got yourself in a heap of bullshit, Mr. Walker. I mean Mr. Crack Dealer. Now, with your record, you can easily get twenty years under the Career Criminal Statue for the weapons that happen to be stolen. And the assault on the confidential informant Daniel Williams can get you ten years alone."

I couldn't believe this shit. This nigga Bud was the people! I knew it was over at that moment.

"Walker, we already know you're not the man. So, with that being said we gonna give you a chance to save yourself, and go back home to that big booty girl you got," the agent said with a sly grin on his face.

My jaws tightened from the blatant disrespect.

The agent continued, "All we want is your Uncle Ricky and you walk, just that simple."

I couldn't believe the audacity of this cracker that sat in front of me. Not only did he want me to snitch, but he wanted me to snitch on my family, my blood family at that. A nigga that's been looking out for me since I spoke my first words. Never would I betray my mans. I would die for the cause if need be. The feds had me fucked up in a major way and for the disrespect, I spit in the agent's face. Watching the phlegm slide down the side of his face, I laughed.

"Snitch on Rick! You got me fucked up crackers!" I laughed at him.

He rushed me landing blow after blow to my exposed face, calling me everything but a child of God.

After taking my ass-whooping, I was taken to solitary confinement, swollen face, and all. I still felt like the soldier I was raised to be. I would never let them break me physically or spiritually. This nigga Bud had penetrated my crew on some Mickey Mouse shit, but trust and believe he would be punished for his federal acts. The feds had nothing on me with the drugs, nothing but their informant's word. Bud hadn't gotten a chance to set me up with the work which was a blessing, not to mention Bud was nowhere to be found.

Five months later, I was sitting before the Honorable Judge Chambers, a Federal Judge. I was about to get sentenced by the United States Government for possession of a firearm by a felon. My sentencing guidelines placed me between sixty months to one-hundred and twenty months in Federal Prison. The District Attorney made it seem like I was some heartless gang banga that was terrorizing the State of Tennessee. All the bogus shit she was saying went in one ear and out the other. The only thing that broke my heart was watching the tears fall from my daughter's face, I was crushed. For her to see me shackled and handcuffed like some animal would be forever embedded in my mind.

My court-appointed lawyer could do nothing in my defense. I was caught red-handed with the .45 and the pair of trey eights had my fingerprints all over them. So, it was time to face the music. After the DA did her thing it was now time for the Judge to impose my sentence, but before she did, she asked me did I have anything to say to the court. The Judge wanted me to beg the court for mercy. Not on my clock. I stood up and straightened the pants leg of my Tom Ford slacks.

Turning my back to the Judge, I stared into my daughter's innocent eyes and said, "Precious, Daddy is sorry for putting you through this. I love you with all my heart. I need you to stay strong for Mama and Granny, okay?"

My daughter, even though she had no understanding of the situation I was facing, nodded her head, letting me know my lil princess was a soldier.

"Tammy, you already know my heart beats only for you. I promise I will return a better man. I love you, shorty."

My baby mama was as strong as they come, but not even her strong loyalty could stop her from shedding tears. After sending my love to my family, I turned back to face the government.

"Well, okay, Mr. Walker, now that you have your affairs in order, let's get back to the situation at hand. I totally agree with the

District Attorney. You definitely have an extensive criminal lifestyle. You have been involved with guns, robberies, and habitual marijuana use since you were thirteen years old. You have a gang-affiliated history which, I find disturbing. You have been incarcerated in the State Prison in the past and you still haven't learned that your lifestyle will not be accepted in our community. On count one of your indictment, possession of a firearm by a felon, I sentence you to one-hundred and twenty months to be served in the Bureau of Prisons, the court is adjourned." The Judge slammed the gavel and just like that, I was sentenced to a decade in the feds.

It was crazy how drastically your life could change for the worse in a matter of twenty-five minutes. The bailiffs escorted me out of the courtroom. On my way out I looked over at my loved ones only to see my baby mama and daughter in tears. The only thing I could do was mouth the words, *I love y'all*, leaving them to fend for themselves as I prepared to start a hell of a journey.

Chapter 10

Kilo

Ten years later, and I'm still serving time. The crazy part about it, I was supposed to have gone home fifteen months ago. I was scheduled to be released from the United States Victorville prison in California until a lieutenant tried his hand. You see, since I have been locked up, my so-called loyal baby mama decided that ten years was too much time to wait for me and ended up fucking with another nigga, got pregnant, and eventually got married to the lame. I was sick. I tossed and turned many nights thinking about how another nigga was fucking my baby mama and playing daddy to my daughter.

The shit hurt like hell. It took me a minute to get over it. I had to move forward with my life, as to stand still, is to die. I couldn't remain mad and in my emotions. How could I? I made the choice I made that resulted in my incarceration, it is what it is. My daughter is twenty now and has a child of her own, a little boy.

Yeah, that's right, I'm a proud grandfather. Me and Precious have a strong bond that can never be broken, not even by the feds. It crushed her that I wouldn't be coming home when I was supposed to. I had to explain to her in detail what happened, and it took time for her to understand my situation. So, I had to be patient with her.

The incident went like this—being that I had no support system out there. I mean Ricky would extend his hand when need be, but I was the type of nigga that didn't like asking people for shit. Plus, I owed Uncle Ricky for two bricks. He wasn't tripping, but still. I was going to have to fend for myself and the only way to do that was to hustle. Being a hustla ran in my blood so I picked up the sac. The feds were just like the streets, flooded with drugs, so I got to it. I was doing well for myself.

My locker stayed full of commissary. My account had a few stacks on it, and I was able to send money to my Mama to help with the bills, from prison. It was a Friday afternoon and they had just called the 12:30 recreation move. I was supposed to be meeting this

Mexican Mafia dude by the name of Grasshopper to sell him a gram of heroin. He had already sent four hundred dollars to my account, so I was trying to get to him so I could give him his product. Walking up the walk en-route to the yard, I was stopped by Lieutenant Bivins. Bivins was a complete asshole and was always harassing inmates, the dude was trouble.

"Aye, you, come here," he said pointing at me, signaling me out from the crowd I was walking in.

"What's up, Bivins?" I asked respectfully, thinking about the five grams I was carrying.

"Let me see your I.D."

I got my identification card from my back pocket and handed it to Bivins.

"Kaliel Walker, I have orders to take you to the unit to strip search you."

"Strip-search me for what?" I asked him.

"Don't ask no questions—now let's go," Bivins said, stepping into my personal space.

I had been in the penitentiary for a while and I knew this wasn't protocol. There was no way I was letting this cracker take me in a cell and strip search me. I didn't know what kind of faggot ass shit Bivins was on, but he had me fucked up. I wasn't going—not even at gunpoint.

"You a lieutenant, take me to the lieutenant's office if you want to strip-search me. I'm not getting searched in no cell," I informed him.

"Alright, you wanna do this the hard way, huh?" Bivins said and grabbed me by my tan khaki shirt like I was a child. "I said let's go, nigger," he sneered.

I swung a right hook that connected with Bivins' jaw breaking it on impact. Bivins hit the ground with a loud thud. I blacked out, stomping his head with my prison-issued boots until the guard tower saw me assaulting him and hit the deuces. Correctional Officers came running from everywhere to stop the punishment I was inflicting on lieutenant Bivins. After being apprehended by the C.O., I was escorted to S.H.U, Special Housing Unit. Did I feel guilty for assaulting Bivins? Fuck naw! Fuck Bivins. He violated me in the worst way, and I did what I was supposed to do as a man. When I thought things couldn't get worse it did.

"Inmate Walker—FBI," the tall lanky agent said on the other side of my cell door.

The administration at U.S.P Victorville had charged me for the assault on lieutenant Bivins and sent my case to the FEDs. Eight months to the door and I was handed a fresh indictment. In my mind I was right. Bivins had put his hands on me first. I was protecting myself. The Federal Government offered me a plea for sixty months. I told my court-appointed lawyer to tell the DA I said, *"Ain't no fucking way!"*

I laced my boots up like a soldier and went to trial. If only I would have known the feds didn't have a self-defense law, I would have run with the sixty months, but instead, I went to trial and lost. For playing ball with the feds, I was rewarded ninety-two more months, seven more years with the feds. The trial only lasted a week. Watching the tears roll from my daughter's eyes and the disappointed look on my mother's face made me sick to my stomach.

Only eight months to the door and the jaws of the Federal Government had swallowed me whole and left me in the belly of the beast. Once my trial was done and over, I was told I was being transferred to the notorious, Lewisburg Penitentiary in Lewisburg, Pennsylvania. The horror stories I heard about Lewisburg would make Victorville look like Disney World in Orlando, as I would soon find out. My bus pulled up to the prison on a Thursday. I can remember it like it was yesterday. The clouds were dark grey, thunder and lightning cracked through the sky and the rain poured down on the small country town of Lewisburg.

The prison reminded me of some historic castle that I had seen in a book in Social Studies when I was in eighth grade, straight up. The bus was full of inmates waiting to be shuffled into the gates of hell. Standing at a distance of Lewisburg Prison was at least ten correctional officers with black jackets that had *B.O.P* in big bold letter on the back of them. Not to mention, neither of them was black, Hispanic, or any other race for that matter. They were all

Caucasians, rednecks with a mouthful of chewing tobacco. I knew at that moment I was in for a rude awakening.

"When I call your name, step to the front of the bus," the chubby C.O. said with authority. "Larry Buckley, Charles Winston, Kaliel Walker."

Hearing my name, I made my way to the front of the bus. After being escorted into the prison I was stripped down and handed my prison uniform, mug shot taken and led to a small room that had no windows, just a sink and a toilet that had probably been there since the prison was built one hundred years ago. The room was cold and had a damp and rusty smell. I overheard guys talking on the bus about how all the infamous mobsters had at some point in their criminal history, made a trip to Lewisburg Penitentiary. It was a possibility I was sitting on the same bench that Al Capone had sat on. My thoughts were broken when six big ass C.O.s entered the room, all no less than 6'1 and 200 pounds.

"You're the one who smashed the lieutenant in California?" The biggest one asked, spitting chewing tobacco on the ground in front of me.

I knew this was coming when I was in the S.H.U in Victorville. A guy who had been in Lewisburg told me the guards were known for beating up inmates, especially those sent to Lewisburg for assaulting staff. I just hoped and prayed they would give me a fair one, with handcuffs on I had no chance at all.

"Yeah," I replied

"Was he white or black?" The C.O. inquired.

"He was your color," I responded.

"How big was he?"

"He was about your size," I retorted. A smile came across the C.O.'s face.

"You think you can do to me what you did to him?"

"If you did to me what he did to me," I answered, knowing they was about to get on some bullshit with me.

"So, what did he do to you, Walker?"

"He put his fucking hands on me, that's what he did."

The C.O. stepped closer, invading my space, and said, "You listen and you listen good. I read the S.I.S report and it seems like you like putting your little black hands on our staff. Now, I have a right mind to give you a Lewisburg welcoming and trust and believe you don't want that boy. But we been under a little scrutiny from the higher-ups as of late so you get a pass, but things will blow over. Now, that lieutenant you put your hands on happens to be a good friend of mine. I owe him at least this." The C.O. punched me in my nose, sending me to the cold floor. Blood spilled from my nose profusely. The tight handcuffs cut into my wrists as I struggled to get back up.

"Welcome to Lewisburg, you, black son-of-a-bitch, and make sure you send this piece of shit to D-house or as we call it—Dog House."

That was my first night in Lewisburg. I had transitioned into the prison well, though. Lewisburg was a different kind of prison with a different breed of inmates. Most inmates serving time were sent there for disciplinary transfers. Lewisburg penitentiary was the last step before you went to A.D.X in Florence, Colorado, a 24-hour lockdown underground. Violence and riots were prone in Lewisburg, and only the strong survived. By me being a three-star branch elite for the Vice Lords' organization on the streets, my gang ties and authority within the gang followed me to prison, and once I landed in Lewisburg, my homies, the Vice Lord's, awaited my arrival.

One of my homies, who went by the name K.D., ran the Vice Lords in Lewisburg when I got there. He was light-skinned with long dreads and a five-pointed star tatted above his left eye. K.D. was from the notorious streets of the Westside of Chicago, off Cicero and Monroe. I knew K.D. from another prison in Terre-Haute, Indiana. K.D. was my mans and I was happy to see bro.

K.D. was serving three life sentences until his lawyer found some loopholes in his indictment and got the Ls off his back. Now he only had a twenty-year sentence. To say he was blessed would be an understatement. K.D. told me once I got to Lewisburg that the Vice Lords rolled with the GDs and BDs in a coalition, which was new to me cause in our State Prison they were considered our opposition, but the feds was a different level and it wouldn't take long for me to figure that out.

Me and K.D. were involved in a spade game with two cats from D.C. In Tennessee, spades and dominoes were our thing, so most niggas in our State were good at it. It was evident, how me and K.D. was punishing these dudes. K.D. had felt like gambling and asked me to be his partner. Me coming from a gambler's bloodline, I agreed. Five games later, we were up sixty books of stamps, two hundred dollars in penitentiary currency. The game was intense.

We were playing two-set games, meaning if you got set twice in one game you lost. The DC dudes, who went by the names of Shorty Slim and Mario, went eight and we went five. The outcome of that hand was then making 7, they came up a book short, thus causing them to get set a second time in one game losing again.

"That's two sets, Joe—game!" K.D. said shuffling the cards.

"Alright, run it back, Slim," Mario said.

"Yeah, that's cool, but y'all need to go get them stamps."

"We got you, Moe, deal the cards," Shorty Slim said with a sneer.

"Don't got me—get me," K.D. retorted nonchalantly.

"You know what, Slim, I'm cool." Shorty Slim stood from the table as well as Mario.

"Just make sure you bring my money back. I'll be right here," K.D.'s tone was now more serious and assertive.

Shorty Slim turned to K.D. and said, "Get it how you live, Slim." He put his hand in his pocket, Mario followed suit.

K.D. smiled then rose from his seat and reached in his pants pulling out a jailhouse shank.

"What's good, Joe? Y'all niggas trying to work?" K.D. said through clenched teeth.

Shorty Slim and Mario then pulled out knives. I stood next to K.D., nervous as hell. Some dudes from Baltimore, Virginia, and Maryland also pulled out weapons and surrounded me and K.D. in the dayroom. I just knew I was about to get stabbed the fuck up until the GDs came rushing the dayroom with knives in our defense. The battlefield was now even. The shit was about to blow until a Muslim, who went by the name Bouncer stepped between the violence that was about to erupt.

Bouncer was an old head from New Orleans who had been down twenty-five years on a heroin indictment, and who had also converted to Islam. Bouncer was both well respected and feared throughout the Federal System. Being from Louisiana, Bouncer also had a major influence with the D.C. inmates as they rolled together as well.

"Malik, As-salamu Alaykum, brother," Bouncer greeted in Arabic to one of the GDs that stood with me and K.D.

I would later know this man as Black Mac.

"Wa Alaikum Assalaam" replied Black Mac and walked up to Bouncer, a Kufi covered his bald head and his beard looked like a lion's mane.

"Malik, what is this situation?" Bouncer asked Black Mac, noticing his people and Black Mac's men with mask of death and weapons ready to spill blood.

K.D. stepped up and said, "This cat thinks shit's sweet. They feel like they don't have to pay what they owe me and my mans. I'm Vice Lord and one of Allah's worse children and I ain't going for it," K.D. said, with ice dripping off his tone.

Bouncer looked at his men. "Put your weapons away," he commanded.

Shorty Slim ice grilled K.D. before he put his knife back in his back pockets. Mario did the same and the rest of their homies followed suit, respecting Bouncer's authority. Black Mac gave the GDs a look where words needed not be explained. Black Mac was a devoted Muslim, but always embraced his first love, the Gangster Disciples. He was their shot caller and in return, they respected his authority.

The GDs put their weapons away. But, K.D. remained holding a tight grip on the sharpened piece of steel, ready to get active.

"K.D., put it away, Ock."

K.D. looked at Black Mac, and then at Shorty Slim. After a few seconds passed, K.D. reluctantly put the weapon away. Silence filled the dayroom as the aggression level was high.

Black Mac was the first to break the silence. "Bouncer, we both know being Muslim that Allah does not want us to shed our brother's blood. Allah is all-merciful." Bouncer nodded in understanding. Black Mac continued, "Now I know your men ain't ducking no rec. As my men ain't ducking no rec, but we are still standing here, and nobody is bleeding."

"Yet!" Shorty Slim taunted.

Bouncer gave him a look as to say *shut the fuck up*. Black Mac ignored Shorty Slim's subliminal remark.

"Like I was saying, by us standing here only means one thing. We are here for a solution. This situation does not have to end in bloodshed," Black Mac said eyeing everyone involved.

"Me and dude was gambling, he lost and told me to get it how I live. So, if he not trying to pay me, I'm trying to do just that, I'm trying to see that shit," K.D. said meaning every word.

Bouncer turned to Shorty Slim. "You owe this man and said you weren't going to pay him? You are willing to crash us out on some crud ball move like that? That ain't no man shit, Slim. Either you pay that man, or you see that man," Bouncer said.

K.D. started rubbing his hands together in anticipation of violence.

"It ain't even about the money no more, it's about the disrespect. I'm trying to see dude with that knife," K.D. said noticing the nervousness on Shorty Slim's face.

At that point, K.D. knew Shorty Slim was faking with all that killa shit.

In a low tone, a little above a whisper, Shorty Slim said, "Don't trip, Moe. I'ma get you those stamps before we lock in for the count."

Bouncer looked at Shorty Slim with pure disgust. "Malik, don't worry, Ock, things will be taken care of brother."

"All is well, Bouncer, Inshallah," Black Mac responded, then shook Bouncer's hand indicating the conflict between the two groups was now laid to rest.

Later that night, I was introduced to Black Mac and the rest of the GDs on the compound at Lewisburg. Never in my life had I thought I would live to see the day when GDs came to the aide of the Vice Lords. I mean, for them to come to work, it was no playing. Had not Bouncer and Black Mac been there to defuse the situation things would have got bloody real quick. I learned that Black Mac, whose real name is Alex Montgomery was from Memphis, Tennessee. From some projects called Berry Homes. He had been in twenty years for a Gangster Disciple conspiracy and had a life sentence. Black Mac was once a ruthless individual until he found Islam, yet the gangster was still alive and evident in his being.

Me, Black Mac, and K.D. were walking the track of the prison yard.

"So, you fresh in the system, Ock?" Black Mac asked me.

"Naw, I been in for about ten."

"How you get to this raggedy place?"

"I was in U.S.P Victorville and I caught an assault on a C.O.," I replied.

Black Mac shook his head. "Yeah, them crackers out there is something else. They're disrespectful and sometimes all they understand is violence. What they call you, fam?"

"They call me, Kilo."

"Check this out, Kilo. I don't know how they were moving in Victorville, but in Lewisburg Penitentiary the GDs and Vice Lords run together. Whatever beef you had on the town with the guys kill it. Because here, we are all family. The DC dudes, Baltimore, and Maryland roll together. You been in the system for a minute, so you already know how they're rocking. They're trained to go. Everything is all about respect here, and disrespect is not to be taken lightly, feel me?"

I nodded in understanding.

"Now, you see them cats over there sitting on the bench?"

I turned to see where Black Mac was pointing.

"Those are Bloods. It's a lot of them down here. They into a lot of shit, so be mindful of that if you deal with them. Buddy and them on the basketball court, those are the Crips. We cool with them. It's a mutual respect thing with them."

I was listening to Black Mac intensively as he gave me the layout of the prison and who was who until the deuces went off. C.O.s and medical staff went running to Dog House, my unit.

"Oh, yeah, Kilo, it's an unspoken rule here at Lewisburg that if a man calls you out for some work and you don't answer that call, you can no longer stay on the compound. It's a code we live by, it's a code of the Goons," Black Mac informed me.

I was trying to digest what Black Mac was kicking, not understanding his dialogue until they came out with an inmate in a stretcher. That inmate was Shorty Slim.

K.D. smiled at me then patted me on my back and said, "Welcome to Lewisburg Lord. Welcome to Lewisburg."

That was a few years ago when I entered Lewisburg Penitentiary and since then I have become a seasoned vet in politics, survival, as well as patience.

Chapter 11

"Walker, you're getting a celly," Officer Hackenberg told me from the other side of my cell door, as I finished my last set of pushups.

I had been riding single, solo, with no celly for about fifteen months. You see, I was only accepting cellmates that were on gang time like me, one of the homies. If you weren't Vice Lord or GD, nine times out of ten I was going to get you outta there, by chance or by force. It was Tuesday, and I already knew the bus was coming packed with new arrivals.

In the Feds, new inmates were transferred to different prisons throughout the B.O.P on Tuesdays and Thursdays. Getting up off the floor, I grabbed my washcloth, wiped the sweat from my face, and cleaned up around the severely small cell I called home. I got my knife from my stash spot and tucked it in the slit of my boxers for safety. They could be putting anybody in my cell and one thing being in prison taught me, was to always stay ready, so I don't have to get ready.

"Pop cell sixteen," I heard C.O. Hackenberg say.

My door slid open. A dude about my age stepped into the cell with his bedroll slung over his right shoulder. Seeing his tattoos, I could see he was on my time, gang time. Come to find out he was one of the GDs from Chicago. His name was Lil Tony. The dude seemed cool. He was fresh in the system, so Lewisburg was his first spot.

Lil Tony informed me that his paperwork was on the way, which let me know he was living by the same codes I was, silence and secrecy, no snitching. Me and Lil Tony stayed up kicking it all night, talking about Chicago and Tennessee. The next day I took him to meet Black Mac and the rest of the guys. It was at that point me and Lil Tony started our relationship. Two niggas with the same morals and principles from two different battlefields, putting one concept before everything-loyalty.

Part III: The Jungle

"D-House chow!" yelled Correctional Officer Young.

Letting the inmates know it was time for lunch. It was Wednesday afternoon. Lil Tony and Kilo made their way to the chow hall.

"What's the food like in this place?" Lil Tony asked.

"It's the same everywhere in the Bureau of Prisons, my nigga. On Wednesday, burger, and fries, Thursday, it's chicken and on Friday it's some kind of fish. Monday and Tuesday, they be freestyling," Kilo informed him.

"How many of the guys got off the bus?" Kilo inquired, wanting to know if any other homies had come.

"It was a few of us. I know one of them was the guys. He was a white boy, he had a six-pointed star tatted on his face." "Oh, yeah?" Kilo replied.

"Yes, he might be one of the guys, or he might be Jewish," Lil Tony joked, knowing the six-pointed star was associated with the GD's. The two of them stepped into the loud chow hall.

Lil Tony looked around the crowded dining hall. A lot of inmates stared him down with mean mugs on their hardened faces. He could feel the tension in the air. It was so thick you could cut it with a butter knife.

"Why everybody mugging me and shit?" Lil Tony asked.

"Fam, don't pay that shit no mind. They're putting on a show because you fresh off the bus. All that gon' change when these niggas see what table you sit at, trust me."

After grabbing trays that consisted of a lukewarm hamburger and a few soggy French fries, Lil Tony followed Kilo to a table in the far end of the corner of the chow hall.

"What's good, Lord?" Kilo said to K.D. The two of them shook hands the Vice Lord way.

"This one of the guys?" K.D. asked.

"Yeah, he's one of the GDs from Chicago."

"What's good, Joe? They call me K.D., Mafia Vice Lord from out West," K.D. greeted Lil Tony.

"What up? Lil Tony, Murda Block."

The two shook hands and Lil Tony took a seat at the table, in front of a light-skinned dude, with a bald head and gold teeth.

"What's up, family! Stackhouse, GD Clarksville, Tennessee," Stackhouse introduced, extending his hand in greeting.

"What's good with it, G. Lil Tony."

Lil Tony and Stackhouse performed the GD handshake, making a pitchfork with their hands, as a white boy with a six-pointed star approached the table.

"That's fam I told you about who was on the bus with me," Lil Tony whispered to Kilo, who was opening up a ketchup pack to put on his hamburger.

"This the table the GDs sit at?" The white boy asked.

"Yeah, fam. You one of the folks?" One of the GD's named Scrill probed.

Yeah, my name is Hell Boy. I'm from South Carolina."

Scrill motioned for Hell Boy to have a seat at the table.

"What up, folks? My name Lil Tony."

"What's good, G. I was on the bus with you, you good?" Hell Boy said shaking Lil Tony's hand.

Hell Boy was a twenty-three-year-old Gangster Disciple from South Carolina. He was in on a twenty-two-year sentence for a bank robbery and was sent to Lewisburg to serve his time. After eating their meals, the convicts were walking back to the unit when Lil Tony asked, "What unit they got you in, Hell Boy?"

"They got me on C-block."

"You need anything over there?" Kilo asked.

"Naw I'm good, fam, appreciate it though. It's another one of the guys that got off the bus with us, but he didn't come to chow. He said his name is Lil Folks."

"Where he from, G?" Lil Tony probed.

"He said he's from St. Louis."

"Well, tell him to come outside when they call the rec move, so he can meet the guys," Kilo said.

"Alright, that's a bet. I'ma let him know." Hell Boy shook hands with Lil Tony and Kilo and made his way back to his unit.

Later that day, Lil Tony and Kilo walked the prison rec yard. It was 6:00 in the evening and the yard was crowded with inmates. A lot of them were exercising in large groups doing push-ups, Navy Seals, Kick outs and every workout known to man, while others utilized the prison basketball courts, participating in full-court games. Outside of those activities, some inmates stood in groups politicking, smoking, or just plain in the way.

"Aye, Kilo! Aye, Kilo, can I holler at you real quick?" A skinny white dude scratching his neck asked, walking toward us.

"Hold up, Lil Tony. Let me holler at dude real quick," Kilo said, then walked off with the white dude as they talked in hushed tones.

Lil Tony watched intensively and saw the white guy hand Kilo something. Kilo cautiously looked around before he reached in his pants to retrieve something and handed it to the man. The man happily nodded and walked in the opposite direction. Lil Tony was from the streets of Chicago and knew from his street intellect, that Kilo had just sold something to the guy.

"Let's see what's up with the guys," Kilo said. He and Lil Tony walked over to a group of GD's and Vice Lords, that were sitting on a bench kicking the shit.

"Black bitches crazy as hell. I can't do nothing with no black bitch. The only thing a black bitch can do for me is point me in the direction of a white bitch, straight up! When I get out the joint, I'ma find me a white bitch and run her to the ground, like she got hooves on her feet, straight up Joe!" One of the guys named Crack joked as the homies erupted in laughter.

Kilo and Lil Tony took a seat at the bench. Black Mac and K.D. walked up a few moments later.

"What's good with the guys?" Black Mac greeted.

"Ain't nothing, big homie. Just kicking it with the fam," Kilo replied, while he counted a large number of stamps.

"I heard it's some more of the folks that got off the bus. They're supposed to be in C-Block," Black Mac stated.

"Yeah, we met one of them in the chow hall today. They're supposed to be coming to the yard," Kilo said while putting his stamp book in his pocket.

Five minutes later, Hell Boy and a short dude came walking across the rec yard toward the bench.

"That's fam and them right there," Lil Tony said pointing in their direction. The two of them approached the bench.

"What's good, G?" Lil Tony said, shaking up GD with Hell Boy.

"What up, fam. Aye, this bro I was telling you about," Hell Boy said.

Lil Tony knew at that moment it was the same shiesty looking nigga that was on the bus with him.

"What's up, fam, how are you? My name's Black Mac," Black Mac greeted respectfully.

"Ain't shit, what's up?"

"Where you from, family?"

"I'm from St. Louis."

"You getting on count, G?" Black Mac asked him.

"Damn, nigga, you want my social security number, too?" Lil Folks retorted with aggression.

Black Mac was taken back by Lil Folks' attitude but remained calm and in control, a jewel he had learned from one of his old heads by the name of GF – Godfather.

"No disrespect, soldier. I'm just trying to see if you rotating with the family or not. I don't know if you're new to the feds, but that's how the shit go."

"No disrespect taken. I just came from the State joint and in my state, it's every man for himself, not none of this car shit. But I'm with the guys and I'm subordinate to the business and the body," Lil Folks replied calmly rubbing his thin goatee as he spoke.

At that moment I knew Lil Folks was going to be a problem, it was evident in his rebellious attitude. After kicking it in the yard for another half hour, the yard was recalled, meaning all inmates had to return to their housing unit for 9:00 count.

Laying on his bunk Lil Tony was reading an Urban Novel titled, *Trap God* by an author named *Troublesome*. Lil Tony started re-playing and analyzing his first full day in Lewisburg Penitentiary. The homies he met seemed cool. Stackhouse seemed to be genuine and had a humble characteristic as well as Scrill, Crack, and Kilo. He couldn't really get a read on K.D. but felt K.D. moved a little aggressive for his taste. He had taking a liking to Hell Boy, from how he introduced himself to the guys on some real nigga shit and Black Mac seemed to possess leadership qualities.

He respected how Black Mac handled the situation with Lil Folks. Lil Tony knew that being a boss, you had to think for yourself as well as others and move only on the business, never emotion, and Black Mac showed his boss qualities. Lil Tony and Kilo vibed from the jump. Lil Tony was a good judge of character and so far, Kilo was official, but he also knew jail was like the streets, and without warning, friends could easily turn into foe. One thing for sure, he wasn't feeling the St. Louis nigga, Lil Folks, in no form or fashion. His vibe was negative from the first time he saw him on the bus. His whole persona read deception and disloyalty and that was something Lil Tony wanted no part of.

"D-House stand for count!" the C.O. yelled, then walked down the range looking in cells counting bodies.

After he walked by, Lil Tony jumped back on the top bunk and pulled the blanket up to his neck. The lights went off in the prison, ending another night in Lewisburg and captivity. Lil Tony started thinking about the move he saw Kilo put down with the white dude earlier. He had witnessed him making plenty of the same moves on the yard today. He also noticed he had a lot of books of stamps. If his vision was right Kilo was hustling, and hustling good.

Coming from the Jungle of Chicago it was hustle or die and the hustle mentality would forever be embedded in him. Money was his motivation and hustling was the lane he wanted to be in.

"Aye, Kilo," Lil Tony called over his bunk.

"What's up, Joe?"

"Aye, fam, I ain't trying to be in your business like that, but I see you getting to it around here."

Kilo sat up. "Yeah, ain't nothing major, just trying to survive, my nigga."

"Is it worth it?"

"What you mean by that?" Kilo asked.

"You know—is it some money on the yard?"

"It depends on what you're moving."

"What's doing the most?" Lil Tony asked.

Kilo let out a small chuckle before he said, "Lil Tony, I normally don't have these conversations with niggas that ain't showed no paperwork."

"Yeah, you right, my fault fam—but trust and believe my work on the way," Lil Tony said and pulled the blanket over his head.

The more he thought about it the more he knew he was out of line for bringing up drugs in a Federal Penitentiary. A place where thousands of men had received thousands of years because somebody had snitched on them. I hadn't even produced my paperwork and here I was asking about drugs. In his mind, he knew he was bogus.

"Aye, Lil Tony!"

"What's up?"

"Heroin."

"What you mean?"

"You asked me what do the most on the yard. I'm telling you, my nigga—heroin." Lil Tony pulled the sheet from over his head. Kilo continued, "The dope is in high demand."

"How much?"

"Depends on what you copping. I'm a good judge of character and my instincts tell me you ain't no rat, real recognize real. So, I'ma give you the game about this, so listen up."

For the next three hours, Lil Tony and Kilo stayed up talking numbers. In the end, Lil Tony learned that a gram in the feds could be sold for 400 dollars and if broken down he could make no less than 2,000 off each gram. Kilo told Lil Tony that the key to success was to get the drugs in yourself rather than buy it off the yard, that way he could dictate his own hustle and prices as well as manage his own moves. Lil Tony learned about the currency in the prison with the stamps and how to wire money. A lot of dudes who sold drugs on the prison yard didn't have a consistent plug on the dope and the joint would go on dry spells for months at a time.

Lil Tony laid on his bunk playing with numbers in his head, while the other inmates slept. If he hustled the whole ten years of his incarceration, he could step back into society a millionaire. Lil

Tony had what most niggas in Lewisburg didn't—a plug. Thinking of his growth and development made a smile come across his lips. In the morning he was going to call his ace in the hole, his mans, his family, his lil' cousin K.T.

Chapter 12

K.T.

"Slow as pigs can't fuck with me!" I yelled, flooring the gas pedal to my Mercedes-AMG 565, Bloomington's finest struggle to keep up with the cocaine-colored whip with the 6-liter, twin-turbo-charged V-12 under my hood. The blue and red lights lit up the night as I raced down Market Street, with a Glock 17 under my seat. A fleeing and eluding charge was the least of my worries. "I got something for y'all funky ass!"

I turned my Chicago Bulls snap back to the back and swerved a hard left on Market Street. I grabbed my phone from the clip on my Gucci belt and placed a call. Looking in my rearview, I noticed the boys tailing behind me. I started cheesing hard as hell. The phone rang three times.

"Hello," my girl answered.

"Aye, Tiff, look, I'm running from the law. I need you to meet me at the bank on Veterans and Parkway in three minutes."

"K.T. what you do, boo?"

"Bitch, stop asking all these questions and meet me at the bank like I said," I replied, agitated by Tiff's interrogation, and ended the call. "I got y'all asses," I said out loud. I turned my headlights off, then swiftly turned into the parking lot of Lowe's hardware store.

Pulling in the back of the store, I grabbed the gun from under the driver's seat, the half bottle of Cîroc I had been drinking and my keys out of the ignition. I locked the doors, hopped out of the whip, ran to a tool shed, and hid behind it. From my view, I could see cruisers coming down Veterans and Parkway, then turn into the Lowe's parking lot.

"Shit!" I cursed to myself.

Seeing that I knew I couldn't stay a sitting duck, I ran over to a fence and hopped over it landing in some thick mud, destroying my new Balenciaga gym shoes. Coming out on the other side of Lowes, I made my way across the deserted street en-route to first National Bank, where my girl Tiff awaited me.

"Drive shorty!" I said, hopping in Tiff's tinted Yukon Denali.

Tiff had nervousness stretched across her face. She put the truck in drive and pulled out of the bank parking lot, undetected.

That was a close call, I thought as I sunk low in the passenger seat.

Ain't no way I was going to let them pigs pull me over with that pole and the 30-round extension. I was coming from the club, late-night cruising in the quarter milli Benz when I saw the boys jump behind me. I knew I had to get active, so I Mario Andretti'd they ass. The police were always on my ass in Bloomington. My name was ringing hard because of all the money I was getting. Before my cousin, Lil Tony, went to the feds, he schooled me on the dope game, and when he got knocked, he left me his operation.

I moved to Bloomington with my white bitch, Tiff. She has blonde hair, blue eyes, thick in all the right places and not to mention shorty is a rider—as you can see. The dope my cousin put me on with was enough to change my life for the better. It was good dope. Unlike Chicago, in Bloomington, I was able to get triple for my product. Tiff hooked me up with a few of her people and soon after, I had Bloomington in my palms. The money came so fast I had to spend it.

Me and Tiff stayed in a five-bedroom house on the Westside of Bloomington. A Dodge Challenger SRT, a 2018 Range Rover, and a Cadillac Escalade decorated my driveway. Not to mention, the Benz that I had to ditch. Life was good as it possibly could be.

Later that night I laid in my canopy king-sized bed taking a strong pull of some exotic weed I had got from my white boy, Aaron. The moment the smoke evaded my lungs it felt as if something had a vice grip on my lungs and I started coughing hard as hell. For a hundred dollars a quarter, this shit was definitely worth it. As I flicked through the channels on my 70-inch Vizio that hung on my wall, Tiff came out of the bathroom from taking a shower. Her hair was in a damp ponytail and a towel wrapped around her naked body.

I watched her closely as she went to the dresser, got a bottle of Palmer's Cocoa Butter Lotion, and sat on the edge of the bed. I could tell she was still a little pissed about me getting into the high-speed chase. My dumb ass unconsciously left my debit card and state ID in the whip, which happens to be in her name. After the car was towed, they showed up at the crib wanting to know my whereabouts. Tiff was quick on her feet and told them we had an argument and I took off in her car. They told her I had a warrant for my arrest for fleeing and eluding, but whatever, as long as I got away with the pipe.

I took another pull from the blunt and watched Tiff lotion up her thick thighs, then remove the towel to lotion up her juicy, perfect DDs. My dick got hard as Chinese Arithmetic. I put my hands in my Prada jogging pants and started to stroke myself. Tiff's ass was so phat. She bent over and her wet pussy lips peeked out. Scooting up to the front of the bed, I pulled her in front of me by her thin waist.

While I admired her flawless body, she looked at me and said, "You know you make me sick, K.T."

I ignored her statement and passed her the blunt, which she accepted and took a pull to calm her nerves. I stood up and started planting soft kisses on her neck and shoulders, while I palmed and squeezed her ass cheeks, pulling her close, pressing my hard meat against her. She let out a soft moan when I took one of her erect nipples into the warmth of my mouth. I stepped back to look into her blue eyes. Her loyalty to me alone, made me want to bust a nut. I grabbed her hand softly and led her over to the bed.

"Lay on your back," I commanded.

She looked at me with her blue eyes and smirked before she did as I instructed. Tiff took one more pull from the blunt before she put it out in the marble ashtray, that sat on the table, beside our bed. I was high and horny as I parted Tiff's thick vanilla thighs. Her shaved pussy looked inviting, so I stepped to my business like a G, pulling the hood over her clit, staring me in the face. I started sucking gently at first. Putting two fingers in her love box, I began to finger pop her, while I sucked savagely on her clit.

I knew my work was official by the way Tiff gripped the back of my head forcefully, as I tongue fucked her. Her juices coated my face, soaking my goatee. Once she came, I turned her over and told her to get in the doggy-style position. She obliged and arched her back, tooting her big ass in the air. I spread her voluptuous meaty, ass cheeks, exposing her pink, tight, ass hole. Bending down, I licked her from her ass crack, all the way down to her forbidden hole.

"Oh, my God, K.T.," she moaned, as I stuck my tongue in her ass.

After my oral presentation, I pulled off my jogging pants, along with my True Religion boxer briefs. The veins in my dick, pulsating at the sight of Tiff from the back. She looked back at me, her eyes hazy from the weed. My bitch was bad as shit. I entered her tight walls from the back. Her warmth felt like heaven, as I slow stroked her. Seeing her pink pussy lips, gripping my dick like a glove, turned me into a savage. I began to pump my 10-inches deeper, slamming into her, my balls slapping against her cheeks, while I put my thumb in her ass. I was driving her crazy. I pounded my queen out. Her pleas of pain and pleasure and our naked flesh slapping against each other were the sounds you could hear in our master bedroom.

"I'm about to nut, baby," I announced, as I felt myself about to explode. "Ahhhh, shit girl," I moaned like a bitch, as I pulled out and shot my load all over her big ass. My dick glistening from her sweet juices.

She looked at me with a devilish, seductive look before she said, "Now I gotta take another shower."

Laying in the bed naked, while Tiff was in the shower, I reached over to grab the blunt duck from the ashtray and fired it up. I took a pull and thought about joining Tiff in the shower for round two when my iPhone rang on the tablet next to me. I grabbed it, looked at the caller ID, and saw the number was restricted. I sent the call to voicemail. I wasn't into answering unidentified calls. When you are moving like I'm moving, you have to be extra careful. A few seconds later, the person called back. For some reason, my curiosity got the best of me. I pressed send to answer the call.

"Hello," I answered, trying to disguise my voice.

You have a collect call from, Anthony Banks from a federal Correctional Facility. To accept this call press five. To block this call or any other calls from this prison press—

I pressed five with the quickness.

This call will be subject to monitoring—

"Hello."

"What's good, cuz!" I said, happy as hell to hear from my nigga.

"Ain't shit, just maintaining in the jungle. What's up with you? I been hearing great things about you."

"You already know, fam. Just standing on this business," I told Lil Tony, letting him know I was out here playing no games.

"Listen, G, I'm trying to take care of something in here. You know how you out there moving with the defense, right?"

"Yup."

"I'm trying to bake a cake in here. I just need all the ingredients, though. When I get situated, I'ma let you know about the demo. Until then, I just need you on standby. I'm talking about touching that paper for real, tripling the numbers you out there doing."

"Oh, yeah?" I replied, watching Tiff's ass coming out of the bathroom.

What Lil Tony was speaking, definitely had me interested. This nigga was crazy. He was talking about doing federal shit, in a Federal Prison. One thing about it, my cousin was a hustla and it was because of him, I was all the way up. So, I was definitely rocking with him. We chopped it up for about another ten minutes before the operator said, *you have one minute remaining*.

"Alright, cuz. I got you, ten toes down. You make sure you hold your head up in there, I got this out here," I assured him.

"Say less. I'll be hitting you up in a minute—be safe out there K.T."

"Love, fam."

"Love."

Our call was terminated. All that night I stayed up thinking about my conversation with Lil Tony. You can take the nigga out of the game, but you can't take the game out of the nigga. For some niggas was sworn in it, but niggas from my bloodline was—Born in it.

Chapter 13

Lil Tony

It had been two weeks since I talked to my little cousin K.T., about possibly setting up an operation in here, to get some revenue in. If I could get an ounce of heroin up in here, I could crush the yard and come home with a meal ticket. Maybe a few million. My lawyer had sent my legal documents containing my P.S.I Presentence Investigation, my docket sheet, and my judgment of commitment, pertaining to my indictment. In turn, I showed my paperwork to the homies. So, at this point, all of them knew I wasn't a rat, that I stood strong on my case, and that I was an official nigga. After getting cleared by my guys, I decided to take Black Mac up on his offer to get some protection.

I located him in the rec yard where he was doing an extensive workout called, the Furious Five.

"What's good, Black Mac? I thought I might find you out here," I greeted.

"Lil Tony, how are you, ock?" Black Mac got up from doing his pushups and shook my hand.

"Ain't nothing heavy, I just came to holla at you, to see if I could still get one of those thangs. You know it's a little aggressive around here. I need something just in case, so I'll be ready."

"No doubt, family. In an environment like this, a man must protect himself to the fullest extent. Self-preservation is always the law of the land. Just remember brother, you have to move with caution when you carry this. Getting caught slipping with one of these can cause complications for you. They are prosecuting dudes for knives. So, you have to be extra careful homie," Black Mac said. He then looked around and checked his surroundings, before he reached in the front of his pants, pulled out a jagged sharpened piece of steel, length about seven inches long, and passed it to me.

I discreetly slipped the tool in my tan khaki pants to conceal it. In prison, a knife was equivalent to having a gun in the world. I knew how to carry and use firearms, but I had never stabbed a nigga.

The few weeks I had been in Lewisburg, I had witnessed three different stabbings and one of them ended up being a body. I made a promise at that moment I was leaving Lewisburg the same way I came in, with no puncture wounds, I wasn't about dying.

"Lil Tony, let's take a few laps."

Me and Black Mac begin to walk the yard.

"Not to be in your business, youngsta. But the feds must have had a hard-on for you to make you out on the gun case. You piss somebody off?" Black Mac asked me.

"I guess you could say that, fam. I beat some bodies in the state and the feds picked up the gun and maxed me out on it."

Black Mac rubbed his beard. "I see, I see, my brother. This prison is disciplinary yard. Most of the men here are serving life sentences or some stupid number that will condemn them to this prison cemetery. My advice brother, is that you lay low, do your time, stay out of politics, get your mind right, get out and never come back. This place is for savages, feel me?"

"How you get to this yard, Black Mac?" I inquired.

"I crushed a nigga when I was in U.S.P Attwater. The nigga died but they were able to revive him. I was reindicted on assault charges. They knew I already had a life sentence, so the extra fifteen years they gave would mean nothing. They sent me here thinking eventually I would get caught slipping and as you say, get the bad end of the stick."

"Damn, my nigga. What you end up getting life for? If you don't mind me asking."

Black Mac looked at me stone-faced before he spoke, "For sticking to the G-code. My uncles had already put somebody to sleep. Unfortunately, there was a witness looking out the window when the gunshots rang out. The witness notified the authorities and placed one of my uncles at the scene of the homicide. My uncles lived a certain code, snitches get up in ditches. Invading the home of the witness, the family was kidnapped, tortured, and buried alive.

"One of my uncle's DNA was found at the scene and he was apprehended and questioned. I guess his demons started to haunt him. He thought about the elderly lady buried in a salvage yard in

Memphis and told them about the bodies that were buried. To save himself from the death penalty, he snitched on his own brothers, Earl Ray and Big Sam. They were caught, charged with four counts of murder, and sentenced to die from lethal injection. My uncles are still sitting on death row at U.S.P Terre-Haut. My snitch ass Uncle Peewee was sentenced to life in prison," As Black Mac told his tale of murder, I could do nothing but shake my head.

"So, how you get caught up in that?" I asked Black Mac, not hearing him put himself in the crime.

"Because my uncles hid the murder weapons at my house. The Feds kicked my door in and found the hammers that had my fingerprints on them. They also found the half brick of crack that was bagged up in ounces. They indicted me on the drugs and the weapons, a ninety-four-C Charge. With my criminal history, I was facing a mandatory life sentence. The feds could care less about the drugs, they wanted to tie me to my uncles. They wanted me to tell or seal my own fate and get a life sentence. I chose death before dishonor. I chalked it up to the game. Now, I have given Allah, the Most Merciful, my life. He has forgiven me for all my sins and every day I walk in my dean as Muslim."

"That's crazy, fam. Your own uncle told? That's fucked up."

"Lil Tony, the game is fucked up. Stone cold hard killas that got bodies upon bodies have told in the clutches of the feds. Understand, anybody can kill a man, killing doesn't make you a man. It's your integrity, your morals, and principles that define you as a man. Always remember that. And if you don't remember nothing else, never compromise yourself for nothing."

I took what Black Mac was preaching and stored it in my mental Rolodex. Black Mac was a real nigga. Even with a life sentence, he remained in control. He was the same nigga every day and had a positive vibe about him. I was going to make it my business to stay around Black Mac and soak up as much game as I could. It was a true statement- real always recognize real.

Me and Black Mac continued to walk the yard, bonding. We walked past a group of dudes standing on the basketball court kicking shit. They were all from St Louis. In the middle of the crowd was the shiesty ass nigga I wanted nothing to do with, Lil Folks.

As we walked toward the small group Black Mac said, "I need to holler at fam real quick."

"You cool?" I asked Black Mac.

"Yeah, I'm cool. Just hold up for a minute," he replied.

I stopped in stride and watched Black Mac slide up on Lil Folks and ask him to step to the side, so they could rap. Black Mac had his hands clasped behind his back as he spoke. It looked to me as if Lil Folks had an attitude, as his facial expression and body language showed his agitated persona. Black Mac remained calm. I noticed the St. Louis nigga walking toward Black Mac and Lil Folks. The situation didn't look peaceful, so I made my way over to Black Mac.

As I approached, Lil Folks was speaking, "—like I said, I'm getting off count and getting on St. Louis time."

"And like I said, you still have to show your paperwork," Black Mac retorted.

The St. Louis niggas came over and stood behind Lil Folks.

"My brother, we have no problem with you getting on homie time. If you don't want to be around us. Then we don't want you around us. But the fact of the matter is, you are a GD and were on count when you got off the bus. The guys gave you a care package. Now, you want to get on St. Louis time. We don't live by no democracies we live by dictatorships," Black Mac said through clenched teeth, standing on principle.

I guess a few of the homies saw the situation and came over to see what the business was, including my celly Kilo.

Black Mac continued, "Now, this the business, okay. You got a week to get your paperwork, present it to the membership or you have to find another residence. And your St. Louis homies can go with you if they want to interfere with GD business. We can all blow this bitch," Black Mac said, eyeing Lil Folks down with violent intent.

Scrill pulled a shank from the confines of his Khakis, ready to pop off. Black Mac waved his hand, motioning for Scrill to put his knife away. Black Mac knew the St. Louis niggas didn't want any smoke.

"Like I said, you got one week and we coming to see you. Let's get up outta here y'all." Black Mac walked off and we all followed suit, leaving Lil Folks in his thoughts.

He had a hell of a choice to make.

Later that night, Me and Kilo sat in the cell kicking the bo bo. Fam was telling me about Memphis and Somerville and how he had set up there. I had always heard that in a small country town the money was good and the competition was nonexistent, but in my environment—Chi-Raq, we Ward over drug turf, making it hard to get money. Kilo showed me some pictures of his family. My nigga was blessed to have come from a good family. He showed me a picture of a female with the Colgate smile, I couldn't help but stare at the picture, she was the most beautiful woman I'd ever seen.

"Who is this?" I asked. Kilo smiled.

"That's my cousin Tia."

"No disrespect, fam—she's beautiful."

"None taken. That's my heart. She been standing by me my whole bid."

"She single?" I probed.

"Yeah, she just got out of a marriage. She drives eighteen-wheelers. So, she be all over the country and shit—she chasing that bag."

"That's what's up," I replied, looking at the picture for another ten seconds before I passed it back to him.

"Lights out!" the C.O. yelled before the lights went off in the cell, evading the cell with complete darkness, ending another day in Lewisburg Penitentiary.

"Alright, bro, I'ma holler at you in the AM," Kilo said, pulling the sheet over his head.

"In the AM," I said.

I wasn't happy, to say the least. The situation with Black Mac and Lil Folks weighed heavy on my mind. This Federal Politicking shit was real, and I had a feeling Lil Folks was on some bullshit, it was in his eyes. I came from a city plagued with killas and murderers and I could spot betrayal and deceit a mile away. It was written all over Lil Folk's face. Pulling my new weapon from out of my pillow, where I had it hidden, I ran my fingers across its jagged edges. Lewisburg was definitely a lion's den. I had eight years and nine months to serve on my ten-year sentence.

Holding my cold tool of death in my hand I made a silent prayer to God, that I didn't have to use it.

Chapter 14

Kilo

"Work, bro—push that shit!" I said, trying to motivate Lil Tony.

We had been doing two count burpees for the last hour and my man looked like he was about to run out of gas. You see, I've been locked up for a decade, so pushing this concrete was part of my makeup. Being in the U.S.P for ten years, I had to keep myself combat-ready. In these jungles, something was bound to pop off, straight up! We were on the top tier, trying to catch our breath when the C.O. started doing her rounds. Her name was C.O. Jenkins, and she'd just started working at Lewisburg. Did I mention that she was black? The only black C.O. in the whole prison. Shorty wasn't fine but she wasn't busted either. She was about 5'4, thick, had real hair, a lil chubby around the waist, and a nice phat ass.

"I'm about to go hop in this water, fam," Lil Tony said, then went to the cell to get his shower things.

I had another plan. I sprayed some disinfectant on the area, where me and Lil Tony had left puddles of sweat from our exercise. C.O. Jenkins walked past, looking in cells.

When she walked past me, I spoke, "How you doing C.O. Jenkins? You a'ight?"

"I'm good," she responded dryly and tried to keep moving.

I wasn't going. "C.O. it would be a blessing if I could just have a few seconds of your time?"

She stopped, turned around, and with a fake attitude said, "What do you want inmate?" Her fake attitude was see-through, like scotch tape, as she eyed my sweaty tattooed chest.

Bitches loved a nigga covered in tats and this hoe was no different. A hood chick with a good job.

"I just wanted you to know, I saw you pass that kite for those white boys while we were locked down. Just know it's cameras all around this place and not to mention it's some rats lurking around here. You're a black woman with a good job and these crackers are waiting for you to slip, so they can get rid of you. They don't want our people working here. Why do you think you're the only one?"

C.O. Jenkins looked as if she was pondering what I was saying.

I continued to lay my lick down, "Shorty, I just want you to be careful around here. You're a beautiful, black woman with a good job, in a situation that could give you endless opportunities," I said before I walked off, letting what I said marinate.

You see, my thing is getting to the money and I have no problem compromising staff to get them to bring something into the prison. The most they could do is write me a shot, throw me in the hole and transfer me to another U.S.P, where I would try my shot again. When I saw C.O. Jenkins pass the note for the white boy, I knew that she was green. I was plotting and scheming all the way to the shower.

Turning on the shower, I let the hot water run over my body, then started scrubbing the salty water off me as I began to formulate a plan to get C.O. Jenkins on my team and start making some real money. If I played my cards right, I might be able to get some pussy out of the deal. It had been ten long years and I was tired of using my hand, you feel me?

After getting out of the shower, I went to my cell to get dressed. I took care of my hygiene, put on my grey sweat suit and a pair of wheat Timberlands. That's when Lil Tony came into the cell.

"Aye, Kilo? Black Mac sent word saying for us to come to the yard on the next move. He said it's mandatory," Lil Tony said.

Knowing Black Mac, mandatory meant to come armed, so I grabbed my knife and concealed it in front of my boxers. Whatever was going on I was going to be ready to work if it came down to it.

The 1:00 move was called. Me, Lil Tony, and Swift G, another one of the GDs that was on the unit with us, headed to the yard to go meet with the guys. Walking on the yard, we spotted the homies crowded at the bench that we sat on. Black Mac, Scrill, K.D., Hellboy, Crack, Stackhouse, and the rest of the men were posted up with some serious expressions on their faces when me and Lil Tony walked up.

"What's up with the guys?" I greeted, then started shaking hands one by one.

"Ain't nothing, ock. We're about to go holla at this St. Louis nigga. Today is his deadline to have his paperwork," Black Mac responded.

I scanned the prison yard and saw the St. Louis niggas on the opposite side of the yard, about fifteen of them in all.

"So, what's the business? What if this nigga don't have it?" I asked, wanting to know the next move so I could be ready. I didn't like freestyling.

"If he don't have that work then he's got to go. He can walk out on his own or he can get carried out. And we gon' bust them St. Louis niggas too if they want to step in our business. Point, blank, period," Black Mac commanded.

This wasn't my first time putting in work. I was always on the frontline for the guys. I tied my Tims up extra tight. A few of the homies were putting on skullies and gloves—combat-ready. Black Mac turned on his heels and started walking towards the St. Louis dudes, with all of us following behind him.

"What's good, G, you got that work?" Black Mac asked, walking up on them, directing his question to Lil Folks.

Lil Folks spit on the ground. "Yeah, I got it. I showed it to my homies," Lil Folks said.

"We saw his work, the homie is good," One of the St. Louis niggas with long dreads intervened.

"We wasn't talking to you nigga. We were talking to the lil fella," Scrill said through clenched teeth, standing beside Black Mac.

"Yeah, we wasn't talking to you, fam. I'm talking to Lil Folks. So, what's good, ock? You gon' bleed or oblige?" Black Mac said, with ice dripping from his tone, fed up with Lil Folks testing his gangsta.

One thing Lil Folks knew, being a GD, if he crashed out with the homies it would follow him throughout the system, and he would forever have to face the guys. Having thirty years to serve, he would have a hell of a bid, so he chose to play smart. Lil Folks reached in the small of his back and pulled out a yellow manilla envelope, containing his sentencing transcripts and docket sheet, and handed it to Black Mac. Black Mac handed it to Scrill.

"We're gonna go through this and get it back to you on the first move after breakfast. Appreciate you fam for making the right decision. Ain't nothing personal, it's just the business," Black Mac stated, before walking off with Scrill.

I followed suit, glad we didn't have to demonstrate with the St. Louis niggas. But something was telling me this shit wasn't over with. I could tell that Lil Folk's pride was hurt and in prison, a man's pride being hurt could be a recipe for violence.

It was 3:30 in the evening as me and Lil Tony sat in the cell waiting for 4:00 count. My mind was going a hunnid miles an hour, as I thought about C.O. Jenkins. When she locked us in for count, she discreetly gave me a flirtatious wink that had me on ten. I was about to try my hand. I started writing her a short letter. It was either going to be a hit or miss. She was either going to get down with the program or she was going to book my ass for trying to compromise staff. I was already in maximum Federal Penitentiary, one of the worst ones at that, what was the worst that could happen? Exactly. I hit the top of my bunk to get Lil Tony's attention.

"Aye, celly, check it out."

"What up, Joe?" Lil Tony said, leaning over the bunk.

"I'm about to try my hand with C.O. Jenkins."

"Man, stop faking," Lil Tony replied like shit was a game.

"Naw, my nigga, I'm for real. I just wrote this bitch a letter. When she does her round for count, I'ma put it up to the window."

"You tripping—shorty gon book your ass."

"What if she don't? Then, I'ma get her to smuggle some shit in here, so we can get some real money."

"You tripping, my nigga."

"We gon' see who's tripping when I flood this bitch," I told Lil Tony, full of conviction.

Thirty minutes after the count, I saw C.O. Jenkins walking down our range, doing her rounds, looking in cells. When she got to my cell, cell 16, I tapped the door causing her to stop. When she did, I put the note in the window, and she began to read it,

"My beautiful Black Queen, you are in a goldmine. It's plenty of money in here. You just have to fuck with the right nigga. I'm not a rat. I can make us thousands of dollars. I can change your life for the better. You will want for nothing, fucking with me. I'm feeling you, My Queen. Let's not let this opportunity slip us by. That lil check them crackers are giving you, can never amount to your worth. Let me show you your worth.

After she finished reading the note, I leaned into the crack of the door and whispered, "Do you understand?"

She nodded and without saying a word walked off. I then crumbled the paper up and flushed it down the toilet. The seed had been planted. Now all I had to do was sit back and watch the growth. Either the C.O.s was gon' come and take me to the hole or I was about to make an ugly come up.

Chapter 15

The next day, when Lil Tony and Kilo were on their way to the afternoon chow, they ran into Stackhouse, who had a worried expression on his face.

"Aye, fam, S.I.S just walked Black Mac off the yard," Stackhouse informed us.

"What you mean they walked him off the yard? I just seen the homie on the rec yard this morning. He was working out," Kilo replied confused.

"Yeah, I know. Then after rec, I went to the unit and something told me to look out the window and when I did, I saw the C.O.s and S.I.S escorting folks off the yard in cuffs. Man, this shit is crazy," Stackhouse said rubbing his tattooed head.

Kilo stood looking like he was pondering something heavy on his mind before he said, "Let's get up with the guys to see if they know something. Black Mac really don't be on shit, so if S.I.S took him, it must be serious."

All three of them walked to the chow hall. Today was Thursday. The institution was serving fried chicken, so almost every convict in the prison would be in the chow hall. Walking into the lunchroom, what would usually be loud, full of frivolous conversation was now placed with whispers and tension. Lil Tony looked to the left in the direction of where the GDs and Vice Lords sat. Reading their facial expressions, he could tell that something was definitely going on. After getting their trays, Lil Tony, Stackhouse, Kilo, and Swift G made their way to where the guys were sitting and took a seat.

"Aye, y'all hear they snatched Black Mac off the yard this morning?" K.D. asked as soon as they sat down.

"Yeah, what's that all about?' Kilo asked in a hushed tone.

The Bloods occupied the table next to the GD's. Everybody knew Black Mac got snatched, so niggas were being nosey and ear hustling, wanting to know why.

"All I know is a white boy came in the unit and told me. But check this out, on the way to the chow we saw the Captain and I asked what was up with the big homie. Man, the Captain said it's a wrap. Fam ain't coming back to the compound."

"He ain't say why they locked folks up?" Kilo asked.

"Nope, all he said was if Montgomery wants to politick, he could do that shit on another yard and walked off."

"Fam, that shit don't sound right. Mac wasn't into anything."

"You know that, and I know that. It's some fishy shit going on," Stackhouse replied.

"We definitely gon' get to the bottom of it," Kilo said.

"I forgot to tell y'all, a nigga named Goose from Baltimore said he was coming out of medical and saw Lil Folks coming out of the Lieutenant's office by himself this morning."

"Who said this?" Scrill asked.

"A Baltimore nigga named Goose. I fucks with dude, he's in my unit," Stackhouse said.

"Matter of fact, where Lil Folks at anyway?" said Scrill.

Stackhouse nodded his head toward the table where the St. Louis inmates sat and behold there was Lil Folks with his permanent, shiesty, look, tattooed on his face, glancing over at the guy's table.

"Whatever happened to his paperwork?" Lil Tony asked, speaking up for the first time.

"I don't know, G. Black Mac was supposed to go over it, last night and get up with me this morning. Never got a chance. But one thing for sure, ain't no GD's about to be going to holler at no lieutenants without one of the brothers with him. That's just the business. I'm tired of Folks ass anyway. Let me go holler at this nigga real quick," Scrill said, then got up and walked over to the St. Louis table.

"Aye, Lil Folks, let me holler at you real quick, G," Scrill said in a respectable but serious tone.

"What's up?" Lil Folks asked almost in a sneer.

"What I want to holler at you about ain't for everybody ears, it's Nation business," Scrill stated, now gritting his teeth from agitation.

Lil Folks stared him down for a few seconds before he stood from the table and walked off to the side with Scrill.

"Man, what up?" he asked aggressively.

"Aye, G, I don't know what you got going on but we heard you came out of the lieutenant's office this morning, by yourself. Care to explain that?" Scrill asked crossing his arms over his chest.

"Yes, as a matter of fact, I do. S.I.S asked me if I was cool to walk this yard. Apparently, one of my so-called homies dropped a kite to S.I.S saying my life was in danger if I stayed on this compound, which is some police ass shit," Lil Folks said.

Scrill looked at him with a look of confusion. "That shit don't make sense, but we definitely gon' look into it. But for future reference don't go hollering at the people without taking one of the guys with you, that's the business."

"How many times I got to tell you niggas, I'm getting off GD count. Matter of fact, where is my legal work? Go ahead and clear me so I can move around you niggas."

"You know what, G. You don't move or act like one of the guys. You come off as an imposter to me and if it was up to me, your ass would have been out of here. But, unlike you, I'm one of the guys for real and I understand protocol. Something you fail to realize. As for your paperwork, the homie you gave it to went to the hole this morning, but I'm quite sure he will be out soon. So, until then, you being cleared by the folks, is on hold until big homie gets out of the S.H.U," Scrill told Lil Folks, tightening his fist, his veins in his hand now visible.

Depending on how Lil Folks responded to what Scrill put down, would determine if Scrill punched him in his shit, for not adhering to the laws and politics. Lil Folks chose his next words wisely.

"You know what, folks? You got that. Let me know when you're done so I can get my paperwork back and cleared," Lil Folks stated before he walked off, leaving Scrill standing there fuming.

"What the nigga say, fam?" Stackhouse asked Scrill as he took a seat back at the table with the homies.

"Man, G, this nigga on some bullshit. He says they called him to the lieutenant office and told him, one of us sent a kite to them, saying he couldn't be on the compound because his life was in danger," Scrill said picking up his chicken and taking a bite.

"That's bullshit. If that's the case the administration would have had his ass locked up. It's called a threat assessment. Them people ain't playing no games like that," Stackhouse retorted.

"You know this as well as the rest of us. But check this out my niggas. Until we find out what's to this nigga, keep an eye on him. Hopefully, we can get them people to let Black Mac out of the hole. But since he's gone, we're gonna have to reconstruct the chain of command, so everybody come outside on the next move so we can figure it all out," Scrill said taking initiative.

All the men agreed with him to meet on the next move. While the guys continued to eat their meal, Lil Folks sat with the St. Louis cats, silently plotting and scheming. He was playing mental chess with his homies. He only had three years in on a thirty-year sentence and didn't want his pace dictated for the next twenty. He had already made the first move on the chessboard. He was playing to be King of the board once the smoke cleared, that he was sure of.

The 12:30 move was called and the inmates in Lewisburg Penitentiary were released from their assigned units to education, work details, as well as the prison rec yard. Lil Tony and Kilo made their way to the recreation yard. It was a hot humid day in the town of Lewisburg, with a heat index of 102 degrees. It was baking on the prison yard. Lil Tony walked over to the bench to where a lot of the GDs and Vice Lords were posted up. Scrill and Stackhouse stood on the bench to address the men in attendance.

"With all due respect to the other families here, this is a GD function and if you not seven-four, can you please give us a few minutes to get our affairs together? It would be greatly appreciated," Stackhouse said, pertaining to men that weren't part of the Gangster Disciples.

The Vice Lords understood protocol and walked away from the bench to let the GDs handle their business. When it was only GDs at the bench, Stackhouse continued, "Now, are all guys standing here seven-four and have been cleared legal documents official?"

"The nigga Lil Folks ain't out here," Scrill whispered to Stackhouse that was standing next to him.

"He not supposed to be here. He hasn't been cleared. Fuck him," Stackhouse told Scrill, then focused his attention back on the family. "As you all know our leader was taken off the compound early this morning? For what? We don't know, but best believe we are investigating as we speak. We all know the pecking order of the chain of command when he was out here. There is about to be an amendment to the pecking order. The original starting five will move up in position minus our leader. We are doing this in the law of our glorious organization. "So, Scrill is now our active Coach. I will run point, Big Nasty you play center—security. Hell Boy you will assist him and Lil Tony, you gon' hold down D-block. All you have to do is report incidents minor or major to Big Nasty and make sure the guys get a care package when they come on the new. Is there anybody who has something to say about the business that was just laid down? If so, speak now." Nobody said a word.

"All right, that's the business. I want y'all to keep an eye out on the nigga Lil Folks. His status is on hold as of right now. Keep him out of all Nation business and watch the moves he makes on this yard. Y'all see anything suspicious, report it to Hell Boy or Big Nasty—love," Stackhouse said laying down the business.

All the guys shook hands with each other, ending the meeting. The chain of command had been amended. The folks were like a well-oiled machine and in order for it to function properly, all the parts had to be maintained and working, so putting the right men in position was a must.

Chapter 16

Lil Tony

I was in heavy thought as I made my way back to D-Block coming from the yard. I was shocked, to say the least when Stackhouse appointed me a position with the organization. I had been a GD since I was thirteen but I came up in a generation where all the structure was done away with. There was no more dictatorship, and it was every man for themselves. But being in the feds was different and the guys ran things differently than how the guys ran shit on the streets. I don't know if I was ready to hold the responsibility that was bestowed upon me, but I had no choice in the matter. This is what I signed up for when I got in on count.

When I walked into the unit, I saw my celly standing on the range talking to C.O. Jenkins. He noticed me come into the unit and winked at me. This nigga was crazy, fucking with this police ass bitch. The other night when he put that note in the window, I just knew shorty was gonna book his ass. I've got to give it to Kilo, he's got balls of steel. His ambition and drive was strong as hell. His get it by any means attitude was definitely a recipe for success. Today's events had me a little thrown. S.I.S took Black Mac off the yard for nothing. I was starting to bond with the fam, the energy between us was positive, he was gangsta to the fullest.

Being in the feds you are around different calibers of niggas in the game from all over the country. Niggas in DC played the streets differently than how niggas in Chicago did, as Atlanta niggas moved differently than Miami niggas. Lewisburg Penitentiary was nothing more than a cess pool of murderers, drug dealers, and robbers. We were all street niggas. I later found out that S.I.S stood for Special Investigation Service, and when they got your ass, shit was real. The thing that bugged me was, one of the homies knew why they took Black Mac, which was strange to me. But I had a feeling that the nigga Lil Folks had something to do with it.

I didn't understand why he wanted to get off count so bad. The nigga was claiming the M.O.B on the streets, then get to the feds where it's real, and wants to roll with your state instead of with your brothers. Shit like that let me know where niggas' heart at, niggas be faking, straight up!

Walking to my cell, I went past the homosexual named Honey. Honey was from Southeast D.C. Honey was a swole ass punk with biceps like the deceased Crip gang leader, Tookie Williams. Even though Honey was on ass, it was known throughout the system that he had hands like Floyd Mayweather. He was also known to put that knife in niggas. Honey had a life sentence for murder and wasn't playing any games. When I walked past, Honey was doing the nigga name KC's dreads and greasing his scalp and shit.

The nigga KC was from Beloit, Wisconsin, he was a light-skinned, fake, swole dude who had just transferred from some federal prison in Wisconsin, for getting caught with a cellphone. The nigga only had sixty months for getting indicted on some heroin charge and he was crying about that. KC was one of those niggas who be lying just to kick it and was always walking around talking behind niggas back and gossiping like a little bitch.

The nigga walked around like he was the realest street nigga alive, but here he is in a maximum Federal Penitentiary getting his hair done by a punk. Prison was definitely a world within itself. Soon as I walked into my cell, my cellie walked right in behind me. He was smiling hard as hell.

"What you smiling about, my nigga?" I asked him.

"Bro, you seen me hollering at shorty?"

"Yeah, I seen you. What's up with her?"

"My nigga, she said she was with the demonstration. I asked her if she would bring me some dope in here. I said if she would, I would give her five thousand up front and another five after we dump the work, but we got two problems. First, I don't have the five gees, and second, I don't know how we can get the dope to her," Kilo said rubbing his hands together.

He was so excited. My nigga was shaking like he had the flu or some shit. The crazy part is I was equally excited. Kilo said we had two problems, but in actuality, we didn't. I could get K.T. to give

C.O. Jenkins the five racks and the work, not to mention my cousin was already on point.

"Kilo, you sure you can trust this bitch? Don't just be on some thirsty shit, because I can get her the money and the work. But I will be involving my people and I ain't trying to get my people jammed up on some goofy shit, feel me?" I told him.

Kilo gripped the bottom of his chin like he was thinking hard as hell. "Alright, listen, bro, this is what we gon' do. We gon' try our hand with some lightweight shit first. I'ma tell shorty to bring us a can of Burglar tobacco. That shit cost like twenty dollars from the smoke shop, that's like a pound. We can make sixty caps off a pound and sell each cap for sixty dollars. That's like thirty-six hunnid if we sold all weight. That's a hell of a flip for just twenty dollars, don't you think?

"But to make shit sweet, if we can get her the five gees up front, she gon' see we ain't playing no games. Once she brings the tobacco in, then she all the way committed. She couldn't turn back if she wanted to, she's already compromised her job. We got the gun to her head, feel me? Then we press her to bust the move for the dog food, just that simple," Kilo said like he figured out a million-dollar trivia question.

What he said definitely made sense. If the C.O. was on some bullshit, then she would book us on the cigarettes. I would rather get knocked for some tobacco than some Dino any day. Thirty-six hunnid off a dub was a crucial flip. I had always heard it was money in the feds but got damn! I don't even know what they call that kind of flip if they even had a name for it.

"Alright, Lord, I feel you. We just gon' have to be extra careful and keep these niggas out of our business. I'ma get up with my people on my end and let them know to be ready. All you have to do is give shorty the phone number I'ma give you and have her call my people who is going to give her the five racks. When she comes through on her end, then we proceed, bet?" I told Kilo.

"That's a bet, bro," he agreed ready to get to the money.

I wrote down my cousin's number on a torn-off piece of paper and gave it to Kilo, so he could give it to C.O. Jenkins. Then, I left my cell to go call K.T. and put him on point about the call he was about to receive. On my way to the phone, I had to walk past Honey's cell, as it was only two cells down from me and Kilos. Honey had the towel covering the cell window, he was probably doing some faggot shit, which he was known to do. I just shook my head.

Once I got on the phone, I dialed K.T.'s number. My nigga answered on the second ring. After the voice recorder went off, letting us know the call would be subject to monitoring, I got straight to the business. I gave him a brief coded synopsis of the play I was trying to put down. What I like most about K.T. was, he never asked questions, he just followed orders. While hollering at K.T., I caught something out of my peripheral vision. KC was sneaking out of Honey's cell.

The dayroom was loud. A lot of inmates were making their way to their cells to lock in for the 4:00 count. I guess KC used this time to discreetly make his move out of Honey's cell, looking like Junior in Menace II Society, when he came out of his cousin's house to go and confront Cain. I just looked and laughed at his gay ass. After talking to K.T., I went back to my cell to let Kilo know everything was a go. All he had to do was give shorty the number and if she stood on that business, we were about to get paid.

The next day I went out to the rec yard to get my exercise on. It was 1:30 in the evening and the sun was out in full blast. I was about to go do my first set when I saw three of the guys walking the track together, but what shocked me was who was a part of the trio. Lil Folks sheisty ass. He was walking with Big Nasty and Hell Boy, the security for the GDs, and to make it worse it seemed like Lil Folks was doing all the talking. I jumped down to do my set of Navy seals but at the same time kept my eye on the three of them. The conversation looked to be serious. I was on my third set when they walked past me. As they did, they lowered their tone to prevent me from hearing what they were talking about. I jumped up from my set and acknowledged Hell Boy.

"What's good, G, what you on?

"What's up?" he responded dryly and kept it moving.

Now, me and Hell Boy weren't the best of friends, but we were cordial to the point that how he just responded was offbeat. Big Nasty didn't even look in my direction, and the nigga Lil Folks gave me a fake mean mug as they kept walking. I had a gut feeling that these niggas were on some pure bullshit. Me, being the type of nigga I am, I wasn't about to kiss no nigga's ass, so fuck 'em. I continued to push up the concrete until they called yard re-call, meaning that all inmates would have to go back to their assigned unit for the count. On the way toward the gate, I saw Lil Folks hand Big Nasty and Hell Boy something. What it was, I didn't know. But, whatever he gave them put a smile on both their faces.

Chapter 17

K.T.

It was 10:00 at night and I was sunk low in the driver seat of my Cadillac Escalade, behind tints. I was watching the Beefee's Gyro restaurant on the North side of Bloomington, and for good reason. At midnight, Heath had run off with one hundred grams of heroin that I fronted him. Word got back to me that he was hustling out of The Gyro spot on the North side. After watching the restaurant for a few days, I knew my source of information was true. The nigga was over here getting plenty of money. The traffic around the establishment was booming.

He thought he had all the sense. He would post up in the restaurant and when the fiends pulled up, he would come out of the restaurant, hop in their whip and serve them. I was fronting this clown grams at $100. So, he owed me ten stacks. I wasn't even tripping about the paper anymore. I had the best dope in the city. I was cutting my shit with mannitol and sometimes fentanyl stretching my dog to the max and it was still a nook. I had over twenty niggas in Bloomington buying one-hundred grams or better, so best believe I was eating. But this situation with this nigga Heath was personal.

Not only did he run off with my shit, but the hoe ass nigga was posting shit on social media, saying he robbed me, that I was a clown, and some more shit. Even though I'm from Chi-Raq, the murder capital of the world, I try to conceal violence and pursue the money. But since I moved down here to Bloomington, I'm starting to see more and more that these niggas are hatas. You see, I'm playing with a bag. I've got a lot of shit going on that's conducive to my finances, so I'm really worth too much to be out here beefing with these lames. But I have to lay a demonstration down in the streets to let him know its levels to this shit.

My bitch Tiff has a nephew. He's about twenty years old. When I say Shorty is a goon, I mean just that. Shorty play's with those poles like he was born and raised on the Southside of Chicago. That's why I recruited him as my lil shooter and gave him ten stacks to spark Heath's ass. I had just sent him a text letting him know I had a visual on the target. Now I was just waiting on him to slide through and put work in. I was gonna watch this shit like an episode of Power. I wanted to see that hot shit go up in him. All I was missing was the popcorn.

As I waited to witness Heath's execution, I started to replay the conversation I had today with my cousin Lil Tony. Fam told me his baby mama was gonna call me. I was supposed to meet up with her and give her five stacks for a lawyer. This nigga ain't got no kids, so you know he ain't got no baby mama. I had to read between the lines. I just knew some bitch was gonna call and I was supposed to give her some bread. Lil Tony said shorty would give me more details about the case.

Whatever Lil Tony had going on had to be big. Five gees was light weight, but it wasn't chump change either. Lil Tony was always plotting and scheming. I missed my nigga to death. I'm just glad he got them bodies off him. When he came home, I was gonna welcome him back like Ace did Mitch in *Paid In Full.* Keys to a brand new Benz and no less than 500k in dead white men. That's on me! The thoughts of my loved one was broken, when I saw this mark ass nigga come out of the restaurant, then hop in a Trans AM to serve a fiend.

Fuck this nigga Kevin at? I thought, pertaining to Tiff's nephew.

I studied my surroundings and saw a masked individual creeping on the side of cars that lined the street of the restaurant. It was show time! I began to sweat under my Dior t-shirt, as Kevin stealthy made his way to the front of the restaurant. The anticipation was killing me. Kevin was only two cars away from the Trans Am when Heath hopped out and the Trans Am pulled off. Heath had his back turned, counting the money he had just made from his serve. As he made his way back inside the restaurant, Kevin made his move and rushed Heath, his pole extended in front of him.

Boc! Boc!

Heath never knew what had hit him. The slugs tore through his back only to exit out the front. The white piercing pain was excruciating. The power from the .45 forced him to land face-first on the hot summer pavement. Just when I thought it was over, Kevin put the foe nickel to the back of Heath's melon and squeezed.

Boc!

I watched as the powerful handgun jerked in Kevin's hand. He took off running down the dark street, leaving Heath a spirit and his brains leaking out of his medulla. Seeing Heath's lifeless body on the ground gave me a feeling of power. Money made you powerful only if you knew how to use it, and I had plenty of it and a loose screw shooter that was addicted to drama. These niggas in Bloomington had better stay in their lane or in the words of the late Biggie Smalls, *"It's gone be a lot of slow singing and flower bringing."*

Chapter 18

Kilo

It was 12:30 in the afternoon when the move had just been called for us to go to recreation, school, or any other programs that Lewisburg had to offer. Today was Friday, so almost everybody was going out to the rec yard, everybody except me, I had other plans. C.O. Jenkins was working our unit today, so I was going to try to holler at her privately without niggas being all in our business. Niggas in prison were nosey as hell. Once the move was over and the unit had been cleared out, I started to take everything out of my cell and put it on the range so that in front of the cameras it would look like I was just cleaning my cell. I knew C.O. Jenkins would be making rounds in a minute and when she did, I was going to make my move. Five minutes later, I was wiping my floor down when C.O. Jenkins made her round. I got the number Lil Tony gave me and balled it up to the point it looked like a small pebble. As she walked down the range switching her wide hips, I got into position.

"What's up, Mr. Clean?" she said once she got to my cell and stopped.

"What's up with you, Ms. Jenkins, you a'ight?" I asked her, nodding my head toward my hand as I twiddled the pebble between my fingers.

She reached her hand in the cell and I dropped it in her palm. She smiled at me seductively before she said in a low tone, "Since I'm doing shit for you. What you gon' do for me?"

"What you mean, shorty?" I'm already giving you a five-piece spicy. What else you want?" I inquired, thrown off by how she was coming at me.

She looked me in my eyes then down to my crotch. "I wanna see that chocolate snickers," she replied with a serious expression on her face.

I looked at her like she was crazy. "Is you playing?" I asked her, making sure she wasn't trying to book me on a 205 shot.

A lot of weird niggas in the feds had that gunning shit bad, jerking they dicks off to female C.O.s. I wasn't no gunner, but this bitch had just asked to see my joint.

"I'm not playing. Let me see something, Walker."

Seeing that she was persistent with her request, I reached in my pants and pulled my dick out. C.O. Jenkins looked around to make sure nobody was watching before she reached into my cell and grabbed my cock, then started stroking it. The freak bitch had her eyes closed and was licking her lips as my joint instantly got hard in her soft hand. I felt like I was going to bust a nut just from her touch. It had been a long time since a woman had touched me like this and her hand felt like velvet.

After she stroked my dick a few times she said, "I see you, big daddy, and don't trip—I got you." She walked off to finish her rounds, leaving my shit rock hard.

I quickly closed my door and put the towel over the window, closed my eyes, and mentally envisioned C.O. Jenkins sucking my dick as I stroked myself. After about ten minutes, I shot my load in the toilet, relieving some built-up tension. After getting my rocks off, I finished cleaning my cell. I couldn't wait to tell Lil Tony about the freak, C.O. Jenkins, and what she had done. Now all I needed was this plan to fall through so we could make some real money.

If this bitch held up her end of the bargain, me and Lil Tony could walk out of the feds millionaires. I just needed Lil Tony to stay focused and out of all the politics on the yard. By the GDs giving him a position of authority, that would be impossible now, because he had to be hands-on with the business. Lil Tony told me a few nights ago about the homie Lil Folks rotating with a few of the guys discreetly. It seemed to me, ever since Black Mac had been escorted off the yard, the nigga Lil Folks been showing his face more often when at first, he didn't want to be around the guys and wanted to be off GD count.

I was Vice Lord and I wasn't supposed to get in GD business, but I had been in the feds for a while now and knew a snake move when I saw one. I could almost bet my release date that Lil Folks had something to do with Black Mac getting off the yard. Shit just didn't make sense. I knew Lil Tony wasn't seasoned in prison politics, but I was going to make it my business to open his eyes to what was going on around him. He was my cellie and I fucked with him hard. Prison was the devil's playground and the deceit and disloyal acts were high as shit.

Since it was nothing else to do on the unit when they called 1:30 move, I made my way outside to the rec-yard to get some air. When I made it to the yard, I went over to the bench to kick it with the guys. When I got to the bench, I noticed that my cellie, Stackhouse, and Scrill were standing off to the side, engaged in what seemed to be a serious conversation. I nodded my head acknowledging their presence, they nodded back and then continued with their conversation.

"What's up, Lord?" I greeted K.D. and shook hands with him and the rest of my Vice Lord brothers that sat on the bench.

"I ain't on shit, just sitting here watching this bullshit," K.D. said.

"What bullshit?" I asked.

"Bro, the folks got something going on. Look around you."

I did what K.D. said and checked my surroundings. What I noticed was a lot of GDs in the middle of the yard in a circle, and in the middle of them was Lil Folks. He had a piece of paper in his hand and it looks like he was reading from it to the guys, something was definitely fishy.

"Aye, y'all, let's spend a loop real quick," K.D. said.

Me and the rest of the Lords started to walk the track. As we made our second lap, Lil Folks and the rest of the GDs made their way over to the bench, where my cellie, Stackhouse, and Scrill were at. Something was about to pop off.

Chapter 19

Lil Tony

I got a message from Stackhouse telling me and the guys to come outside on the 12:30 move, and the message said that it was mandatory. When I got to the yard I was met by Stackhouse and Scrill, they held some serious demeanors.

"What's good, G?" I asked and shook hands with them the folk's way.

"This nigga Lil Folks. That's what's up. This clown has been giving the guys packs of deuce to sell. Nigga ain't even cleared and he hustling drugs on the compound. And what's fucked up is our security know it's against our laws and policies for the guys to hustle without being cleared," Stackhouse vented.

Deuce was a name for K2. A new drug that had hit the compound. It was barely synthetic marijuana. It came on a piece of paper. It was cheap and from what I was hearing, Lil Folks had just flooded the compound with it. He was giving it to the folks in exchange for their loyalty. He was truly giving steaks to the wolves. I looked across the yard and saw all the guys hollering at Lil Folks. An hour later, they called 1:30 move. I saw my cellie Kilo come through the fence and come on the yard.

"Man fuck this shit. I say we run that nigga up!" Scrill intervened wanting to make Lil Folks leave the compound.

"We can't do it like that, fam. In actuality, he hasn't broken any laws. If anything, we tell him he can't hustle until he is cleared, if he bucks then we give his ass physical violation. If he continues with the bullshit, we crush him and get him outta here. We do everything by the laws that govern us, you feel me, G?" Stackhouse said.

What they were speaking on I was slow too, but what I did know was what Stackhouse was on was righteous. I could feel it. Scrill rubbed his thin goatee, pondering what Stackhouse was saying.

"Alright, bro, I'm with you on this. But that nigga Big Nasty, I want him and Hell Boy removed from that security position immediately. The way they flocking to Lil Folks over some K2, and they're supposed to be the backbone of the membership, is a bad look," Scrill said voicing his authority with the Chain of Command.

Stackhouse nodded. "So be it, family." Stackhouse felt the same way Scrill did.

Big Nasty and Hell Boy were not to be trusted, their loyalty was to the drugs instead of the Nation Business. We were about to go confront Lil Folks about hustling on the yard until his paperwork situation was taken care of, but they started walking towards us. The closer we got, the clearer I could see their facial expressions were serious as stone. They formed a circle around us leaving us in the middle. Lil Folks stepped inside the circle with his hands clasped behind his back.

"What's good with the guys?" This nigga had the nerve to say with a smirk on his face.

"What's good with you hustling on the compound? You know you can't get money around here unless you produce some paperwork. Protocol my nigga and that's just the business," Stackhouse told him.

Lil Folks chuckled lightly, "That's the business, huh? Well since y'all so much on the business and know every fucking thing, our Coach was just taken off the compound a few days ago and y'all already replaced his position ASAP. You stepped up in his slot. If you know the business like you say you do then you should know that the only one who can appoint that Position of Authority is one of the big homies. Did you know that? And if so, where is your proof? Because we on the business, right?" Lil Folks asked with a sneer.

Stackhouse chose his words carefully before he spoke, "Our Coach is coming back to the yard, so I took the initiative to hold his function until he came out," Stackhouse said.

"Without authorization from one of the board? You deceived the guys, fam—you bogus," Lil Folks replied as he pulled a piece of paper from his back pocket and unfolded it.

"I have a line on one of the board, Big Cliff. We all know who Big Cliff is, don't we? Of course, we do. He speaks for the table. I emailed him to let him know that the locking clamp in the chain of command was no longer with us due to the administration, and our team here at Lewisburg was in need of an active coach. This was his reply, "*To all seven-fours, we move in the teaching of our great Chairman. Our chain must stay strong with unbreakable links. The starting five must be willing to play their positions without questions from the point guard down. The men in these positions must work tirelessly if we as a body is to move forward in Growth and Development. As of right now, until further notice, Lil Folks will oversee the team to make sure the goals of our glorious team organization are met in all endeavors, P.M.L Big Cliff,*" Lil folks finished reading the printed email, then handed it to Stackhouse.

Stackhouse reread the dreadful words.

"You are no longer our Coach, fam. I'm the coach. This is now my yard. Scrill you are not the point guard either. I will appoint one shortly. Now is there anybody who has something to say about the business that has been laid down by the board of directors?" Lil Folks asked, looking into the eyes of the men. Nobody said a thing. "Very well, that's the business. Now that we got the small shit out the way let's move forward and get to the money. Aye, Big Nasty, Hell Boy, let me holla at y'all real quick," Lil Folks said and walked off with Big Nasty and Hell Boy.

The guys all went in their own directions as I stood there with Stackhouse and Scrill. Stackhouse kept reading the email over and over.

"Man, that email is bogus, G," Scrill said out of nowhere.

"How you know?" Stackhouse said looking up at Scrill.

"G, I was in U.S.P Atlanta with Big Cliff. I was his personal security for two years. Old head don't even speak like this, that ain't his dialogue. Secondly, Big Cliff don't speak for the table, Mac-Slick from Memphis do. This nigga Lil Folks on some bullshit, G," Scrill retorted.

"Do you have an email from Big Cliff?" Stackhouse asked.

"Nah, but I know Black Mac got a line on Mac Slick. How we get it, I don't know," Scrill replied just as Big Nasty and Hell Boy came walking up.

"Aye, Stackhouse let us holler at you real quick," Big Nasty said through clenched teeth.

"What's up?"

"Lil Folks said your service are no longer needed. You got to go, G. You buck we gon' crush you," Big Nasty threatened and pulled an 8-inch rushed bone crusha from his waistline.

Hell Boy pulled his knife as well, ready to get to the violence. Stackhouse looked at me and then at Scrill and back to Big Nasty. Big Nasty was 6'1, 270 pounds, and was serving double life in the feds. He had gotten orders from Lil Folks to remove Stackhouse from the compound, and he was going to do just that. Stackhouse weighed up his options.

If he bucked, he knew Big Nasty and Hell Boy would stab him, and that he didn't want, so he obliged to their dictatorship and made his way over to a C.O., who was standing by the fence to tell them that he could no longer be on the compound. The administration was aware of these incidents where men were forced by other men to leave the prison. The procedure was called getting ran up, and Stackhouse had just got ran up by his brothers, the GDs. The C.O. unlocked the fence to let Stackhouse out the rec-yard, to only escort him to the S.H.U, Special Housing Unit, where he would be held on threat assessment until he was transferred to another prison.

After the yard recall, I left the rec-yard and went back to my unit. Once I was back in the unit, I went to my cell and hopped on my bunk. Today's events let me know I was involved in some serious gangsta shit. Lewisburg was a violent place. It wasn't that I had to worry about niggas from other geographical areas, it was my own homies, the folks. Now with this nigga Lil Folks getting the yard, I knew shit was about to get worse before it got better. I ran my hand over the front of my pants where my shank rested in the slit of my boxers. Something was telling me it was going to be a time when I would have to put it in a muthafucka and that's on the real. I was replaying the incident with Stackhouse when Kilo came into the cell. It was time for us to lock in for the 4:00 count.

"Bro, what was that shit with Stackhouse?" he asked as the C.O. locked the cell door behind him.

"This nigga Lil Folks came out with an email, it supposedly came from one of our superiors, saying he was supposed to get the yard," I informed him.

"What that got to do with Stackhouse getting ran up? Stackhouse's an official nigga."

"He said Stackhouse was bogus because he didn't have the authority to appoint himself overseer, I guess."

My celly just shook his head. "Damn, Lil Tony, y'all were never supposed to let that happen. Y'all haven't even seen that nigga paperwork. I know you new to the system, Lil Tony but these niggas are demons when it comes to this politicking shit. Niggas be having fake emails and some more shit. Dude will do snake shit to get a position of power. I guarantee shorty did some snake shit," Kilo said.

"So, how do I fix it?" I asked him, needing some guidance.

"First, you have to discreetly. Find out if the email is official. You're gonna have to rock him to sleep, make him feel you are loyal to him, and subordinate to his leadership. Conceal your emotions as well as your intentions. Try to get under him. Try to get in a position at the table with him. Become his right-hand man and on the low recruit your own team.

"If that email is bogus then you gonna have to blast that nigga, stab his ass up, get him off the yard, and have your proof to present to the membership to justify your righteous call, after you spill that nigga's blood, and all while getting your money up. This shit like the streets, it cost money to go to war. The only difference in here is it's mostly mental warfare, you understand?"

I soaked up what my celly was speaking on and it was all making sense the more I listened and put the shit into perspective. I felt it in my gut that Lil Folks had just pulled some cornball shit, but he had the entire membership behind him. I didn't know who I could trust. The only one of the folks I felt I could trust right now was Scrill. I needed to find out if that email from Big Homie was legit and if it wasn't, I was going to have to take initiative bringing me a move, but I definitely had to get my money up.

"Aye, what's up with that C.O. bitch? I see she working today," I asked Kilo after hopping off my bunk to stand for the 4:00 count.

Two C.O.s walked past the cell to count our bodies. C.O. Jenkins was one of them. When she looked in the cell, I saw her wink her eye at Kilo as she kept walking.

"Do that answer your question, my nigga?" Kilo said cheesing hard as hell.

"I see you, fam!"

"Naw, you ain't seen shit. Boi, the hoe jacked my dick off," Kilo told me.

"Ain't no way she did that shit," I said not believing him.

"Nigga, on the fin!" Kilo said putting it on gang.

At that point, I believed him.

"But fuck all that, I gave her your people number and she said she got me. So, as long as our side take care of the business and the hoe do what she is supposed to do, which I think she will, we gon' be on, my nigga! We gon' flood this bitch until they get us off this muthafucka. If we can make one-hundred gees a piece, it's whatever with these weak ass niggas. We can blow this bitch, get another yard and do it all over—it's money in the fed," Kilo said.

My side was going to handle that function. KT was already on point. We were just going to have to be patient and give C.O. Jenkins time to make the call. Until then, I would have to be on point around the homies and at the same time conduct an investigation on Lil Folks and that email. The first thing in the morning I was going to get up with Scrill to see if he would aid and assist me in this righteous endeavor.

Chapter 20

Kilo

Shit was starting to get crazy around the joint. The GDs had just run Stackhouse up, with the perception that he was being insubordinate. I knew whatever the case was, the call was bogus. Stackhouse had been in the feds for almost twelve years. A lot of niggas in the system held reputations, some held minor reputations. You had the hot niggas, the ones that testified on their co-defendants and were labeled as rats. They usually got crushed as soon as they landed on the yard. Then you had niggas that held reputations as being a Goon, the ones that pushed that knife in the system, poking niggas up!

They were always getting transferred from prison to prison for spilling a niggas blood for some reason or another. Then you had the ones who were men. They were held in high regard. They lived by righteous conduct that was solid. Stood strong on their case and lived by the G-code and Stackhouse was one of those men. His name was gold in the feds. Whatever the matter, I knew it was bullshit that happened. I was Vice Lord so I couldn't get in GD business, but I was going to make it my business to lace my celly on how this shit was supposed to go.

I refused to let anything happen to Lil Tony. He was a good dude, so I was going to navigate him through the bullshit and hopefully, we didn't have to blow the yard before we got to the money. I had been keeping my ear to the yard and had heard how Lil Folks flooded the yard with K2. His product was making niggas have episodes. Niggas were falling out, throwing up, getting carried out on stretchers and the crazy part about it was the high everybody was chasing. Lil Folks and his crew were getting money. I watched as they made big boy moves on the yard. They would go to commissary and buy all the newest gym shoes.

The K2 brought penitentiary riches, and Lil Folks and the GDs that followed him reaped the benefits. I had even noticed my Vice Lord brother, K.D. following behind Lil Folks. I know Lil Folks was hitting K.D. with the K2. K.D. had a lot of traffic coming to his unit to holla at him for some deuce. One of my brothers named Pistol had informed me that K.D. was hustling. K.D. held leadership position for the Vice Lords in Lewisburg and conducted himself as such, but as of lately he had been distancing himself from the guys, only to choose money. Nothing was wrong with getting to the bag, but you still had to attend the Nation Business and what was going on around you and I was going to remind him of that when I caught up with him.

It was Saturday evening in Lewisburg Penitentiary. I hated weekends in prison. It seemed like the weekend would drag. I sat in my chair watching an episode of Wild -N- Out. I didn't really watch a lot of TV because of the way they had the TVs in the maximum-security prison setup. They didn't have TV rooms, the flatscreen televisions were hung on different poles in the unit. In the Feds, shit was really segregated. The gangs had their own televisions. The white boys, Mexican gangs, along with the DC dudes and other State niggas that weren't gang banging, also had their own TVs.

Me, myself, I wasn't comfortable enough in prison to let my guard down to watch TV all the time, niggas walking behind me and shit. I had been in the United States Prison for ten years and I'd seen many niggas get crushed like that. A nigga would be caught up in watching *Love and Hip Hop*, then a nigga you have been owing two books of stamps for a week creep up and put the knife in your neck. Fuck that! Today was boring as hell, so I was checking the hoes out on *Wild-N-Out.* I saw C.O. Jenkins doing her rounds on the range. It had been two weeks since I had given her the phone number to bust a move.

Ever since then, the bitch hadn't said a word to me or acknowledged me for that matter. How this bitch went from squeezing my dick to not fucking with me definitely had me baffled but nervous at the same time. For all I know, this bitch could have reported me to S.I.S. Nah, that didn't make sense either because they would have come to look me up and wrote me a shot for trying to compromise staff.

That shit was an automatic transfer. I knew one thing for sure, this bitch was on some weird shit. Since she wasn't speaking to me,

I wasn't speaking to her. I wasn't kissing nobody's ass and that was for sure. I glanced at my G-Shock watch, saw that it was 1:25 p.m., which meant they were about to call a 1:30 p.m. move for recreation.

"Fuck it!" I said out loud.

There was nothing going on in the unit so I might as well go outside. It was Saturday so maybe I could find somebody on the yard selling some Shine, also known as white lightning in prison. In Lewisburg, you could get a water bottle of almost pure alcohol for ten books of stamps, that's about fifty dollars in yard money. For that fifty dollars, you could get real nice. Add a packet of pineapple Crush Kool-Aid and you got some Ciroc—the shit is just that good. I went upstairs to my cell to get my knife. After concealing the weapon on my body, the 1:30 move was called. I went to my stash to get some books of stamps and made my way to the yard.

When I walked through the fence to enter the recreation yard the 98-degree summer weather greeted my skin with ill intent. It was hot as hell out here and the yard was in full rotation. I made my way over to the bench to see what was up with the guys. As I made my way across the yard, I could see Lil Folks over there. When this nigga first came down here you couldn't force him at gunpoint to kick it with the guys. Now, this nigga was hanging out like he been around for years. It was funny how money and power could change the characteristics in a nigga, straight up! I greeted the GDs dryly and walked over to where K.D. was standing.

"What's good, Lord?" I greeted, then we shook hands the Vice Lord way.

"Ain't shit, just trying to chase this bag," he replied, pulling out the plastic baggie filled with books of stamps.

I looked my homie in the face and saw that he was high as the moon. His eyes were red as a stop sign. I had never seen K.D. this way, so to see him out here like this in front of the brothers was a surprise. He was all the way out of line as far as our code of conduct.

"Aye, Lord, come bend a few laps with me real quick. I gotta holla at you on some Nation business," I told him, so I could get a one-on-one with my nigga.

We walked away from the bench. As we did, I caught Lil Folks mugging the shit out of me, but what he didn't know was, I ain't like his snake ass either. When me and K.D. got away from the guys, I got straight to business....my approach assertive.

"Aye Lord, you're getting high?" I asked him, wanting to know the truth.

He cheesed at me before, replying, "This shit ain't 'bout nothing. Ain't nothing but a lil deuce," the nigga had the nerve to say.

"Bro, you smoking that bullshit? You don't even know what you smoking. Secondly, you in a position of authority. You are not supposed to be coming around the men looking all spaced out and shit. That don't show strength, that shit shows weakness, and third you getting that shit from Lil Folks. Them niggas ain't even seen his paperwork. Now all of a sudden, he the shot caller? Come on, Lord. You been in the system long enough to know this shit don't go—and you know it don't go like that. Don't let no stamps get in the way of you going by protocol, fam. You know that ain't how we move," I told K.D., hoping he would see the merit in what I was saying.

"I think you wrong about shit that don't concern you, Lord. Lil Folk said his work is official and he gave it to Black Mac before he went to the SHU. One of the higher-ups said Lil Folks was to have the yard. He even showed me the email. Fam is who he says he is. As far as me handling the business with the MOB, shit is getting stood on properly. Me smoking K-2 is not interfering with Nation business. So, it's not a problem. Only when it becomes a problem will I stop. It ain't no different than when you come out here with liquor on your breath. If you gon' be on the business Kilo then be on the business all the time, and not just when it's convenient for you," K.D. said, which aggravated me even more.

"First and foremost, Lord, anything that got to do with Vice Lord is definitely my concern because I'm on Vice Lord. Like I said, them niggas ain't even seen his paperwork. If you conducting business with him and it comes out he's not who he is, then what? It won't just affect you it could possibly affect all of us—and that by law is a security breach. And make me understand how smoking

K-2 is the same as drinking alcohol? That K-2 shit is the new age crack, my nigga!" I said.

"Look, nigga, I said what I had to say. If you feel some kind of way about how I'm holding shit down, then get up with who you need to get up with—it is what it is."

I looked K.D. in his blood-red eyes trying to get a read on him. His energy was completely off.

"You know what, Lord? You got that," I told him and walked off, leaving him standing there.

I went over to the pull-up bar to get me some sets in. I watched K.D. walk back to the bench, then step to the side to holla at Lil Folks. I could see them looking over at me. Ever since Lil Folks had got off the bus it had been some bullshit going on the yard. Black Mac had been on the yard for ten years and as soon as this nigga Lil Folks come down here and the guys ask him about his paperwork, Black Mac comes up missing and Lil Folks got the yard. Then he sends the guys to run Stackhouse up, an official nigga might I add.

Now this nigga acting like he rocking with him. One thing about it, if K.D. didn't get his shit together, he was going to get sat down from his position. I had a line on one of the homies—my own Uncle Ricky was one of our founders. I could have come down here and exploited my juice and took control of the yard from K.D., but I didn't have a thirst for power. I had a thirst for money, and I had an undying love for the Vice Lords. I would be damned if I let K.D. taint the face of our Nation.

Yard recall was called, so we had to return to our units. The vibe on the compound was fucked up, but I was gangsta. I was always taught to think before you react. My mind was focused. All I needed was for C.O. Jenkins to bust this move for me and Lil Tony. Once I got my bag right, then whatever enemies I had on the yard—one by one would come up missing and that's the business on the fin!

Chapter 24

4 Months Later

The weather in Lewisburg was a piercing 2 degrees below, as the fluffy snow blanketed the prison yard at the Lewisburg Penitentiary. It was the middle of December, two weeks away from Christmas. Lil Tony and Kilo were bundled up walking the track. Even though it was cold outside, inmates hit the rec-yard instead of being on the unit with nothing to do. A lot had transpired in the last four months. S.I.S told Scrill that Black Mac and Stackhouse had a threat assessment and would be transferred to different prisons. Stackhouse had sent a kite out to the yard, as well as his Administration Detention Order. The US Department of Justice reason for holding you in the SHU.

It read," *It is the Correction Supervisor's decision based on all the circumstances, that the above, named inmates continued presence in the general population poses a threat to life, property, self, other inmates, or to the security or orderly running of the institution, because of a threat of violence on the inmate's life or well-being."*

Stackhouse informed us in the kite, that Lil Folks told S.I.S he wasn't allowed back on the compound, him or Black Mac. Stackhouse also put in the kite that Lil Folks was a rat and had testified on his codefendants on an armored truck robbery in which one of the employees for Brinks was shot and killed during a broad daylight robbery. All of them were indicted on the robbery and facing life imprisonment. Lil Folks felt that was too much to endure and chose to cooperate with the Federal Government, even telling them where the stolen cash was hidden. In the end, they were all sentenced to life in prison, except Lil Folks, he was exempt. He was only sentenced to three-hundred and sixty months—thirty years in Federal Prison.

Stackhouse also said he was working on getting a line on one of the superiors. He would have it soon and would send it to the compound as soon as he could. Until then, they were to move with caution and the information they now had was not to be exposed or repeated to anyone. They were to utilize silence and secrecy until they had Lil Folks' legal documents and the email from the big homies in their physical possession. Once they did, they were to handle Lil Folks in the proper fashion, pertaining to law and that's exactly what Scrill and Lil Tony planned to do.

"So, check it out, my nigga, Shorty pulled up on me earlier and said she was going to call your people today when she gets off work. I guess she through playing games. So, you might want to call fam and let him know to get ready," Kilo said, then took a sip from his coffee mug.

"Ain't no need to call. He already expecting shorty to call anyway. I raised my nigga to stay ready so he don't have to get ready," Lil Tony replied nonchalant.

"Alright, that's what I'm talking about! Talk that shit to me then." Kilo was geeked seeing that opportunity was about to present itself.

"But aye, I'm 'bout to holla at this cat Lil Folks real quick. I'ma get up with you when we get back in the unit," Lil Tony said and gave his celly some dap before he walked toward the bench, where Lil Folks, Big Nasty, Hell-Boy, and a few more of the men were posted up.

For the past four months, Lil Folks had been shaking the yard with his potent K-2 he was selling. Lil Folks had made it mandatory that the guys sell K-2 in packs, called Nation packs. Eighty-five percent of the profits were to be returned to Lil Folks. Lil Folks was using his position of authority to extort the membership. If all the money wasn't turned in from the Nation packs from the individual responsible, they would get a physical violation, known as a head-to-toe. Lil Tony was one of the guys chosen to sell Lil Folks drugs. Lil Tony didn't like the idea of hustling for Lil Folks, but he had to play his position if he wanted a shot at bringing Lil Folks his demise. The situation Lil Tony was now placed in was a situation of Do or Die.

"What's up with you? You got that for me?" Lil Folks asked Lil Tony, pertaining to the twenty books of stamps he owed for the Nation pack of K-2.

Lil Tony reached in his coat pocket to retrieve the two bundles of stamps. Big Nasty and Hell-Boy watched him through their bloodshot eyes, apparently high off K-2. They looked evil and untrusting.

"Yeah, fam, I got you," Lil Tony replied and handed the stamps to Lil Folks.

He put them in his pocket. "I don't have to count that do I?"

"G, you a grown man. You gon' do what you wanna do," squinting his eyes at Lil Folks.

"You know folks, you got a slick ass mouth. You need to turn the volume down on that shit. Especially when you speaking to authority, you better show some respect," Big Nasty threatened.

Lil Folks laughed lightly at Big Nasty's aggressiveness as well as his loyalty. "Nah, folks ain't mean no disrespect, did you, Lil Tony?" He questioned while staring Lil Tony down.

Lil Tony had to bite his tongue to prevent what he wanted to say from coming out of his mouth. Not wanting to cause complications for himself he chose his words carefully.

"No disrespect intended, family. We the guys, we don't disrespect, that's law."

Lil Folks smiled at Lil Tony, then put his gloved hand on his shoulder. "You know, Lil Tony, it's a drought on niggas like you. Niggas that know how to follow orders. Niggas that don't ask a lot of questions. Our mob needs more soldiers like you. Unfortunately, I don't feel the same for Scrill, that nigga rub me the wrong way G and when niggas rub me the wrong way, I get them from around me. I need you to do me a favor. I need you to keep an eye on that nigga, watch his moves because I have a feeling, he is going to need a change of residence, but a nigga like him not going to walk up top, he gon' buck. So, as you know our literature teaches proper preparation prevents poor performance. You are familiar with the 5 Ps, right?"

Lil Tony nodded his head. "Of course, you are. So, when Scrill jumps his rebellious ass out there. I'm going to have you smash his ass off the yard. But, moving forward, take this, it's one hundred pieces of K-2 in this bag and since you're a good earner, instead of bringing back eighty-five percent—we gon' split this pack in half. You get fifty books and bring me fifty books. You're too valuable to be just a worker. You see Lil Tony, in every mob, it's always an inner circle within the circle. You, Big Nasty, and Hell-Boy are part of my inner circle.

"The organization is not a democracy but a dictatorship. It's the inner circle's job to enforce the laws to the fullest extent. The times have changed with the generation of leadership. The old man is never going to leave Colorado and Big Cliff and the rest of them old niggas can't control the streets from prison. Either way, they are going to change with the times or get left in time. That's just the fact of the matter, G," Lil Folks said, laying down his ideology on Nation business.

Lil Tony took the K-2 and put it in his pocket.

"Don't even sweat it, family. When you push the button just know I'ma be ready to blow his ass up. And as far as this pack, have something ready for me in a couple of days, because this shit gone be gone. I got my unit sewed up. But they about to call this move and it's cold as a hooker's heart out here. I'ma get up with you brothers tomorrow," Lil Tony said, then shook hands with them the GD way.

When he shook Big Nasty's hand, Big Nasty mugged him viciously—blatantly showing his dislike for him. Lil Tony just smiled before he walked off toward the fence, heading back to the unit. He was playing his position to the fullest. All he was waiting for was the paperwork to come back. When it did, he was going to blow Lil Folks' ass to the moon for his insubordinate acts, that was law!

Chapter 25

Lil Tony

Walking back into my unit I was mad as a muthafucka! This rat ass nigga was irking me. In all reality, I was tired of playing with him. I wanted to smash him without the paperwork, but I knew if I did without proof, the guys would blast my ass and it was a possibility I could lose my life in here. He gave me the pieces of K-2 to try to reel me in. He was trying to bake me a cake to run Scrill up which was not going to happen. All me and Scrill were waiting on was for Stackhouse and Black Mac to send in that info. Until then, I was just going to keep my emotions in check and keep playing the square-ass nigga Lil Folks like a PlayStation.

One thing for sure, when the word came down to move, I was going to have to bring Big Nasty a move first with his super tough ass. Hell-Boy would have to go as well. I thought Hell-Boy was a playa when I first met him, but that was just a lesson taught to never judge a nigga too quick because a nigga will switch up. If money or K-2 can make them change and turn against Nation business, then you definitely don't have any place on this compound. I made my way to my cell to get a summer sausage and two soups out of my locker. Being outside I had gotten me hungry as hell. Walking to the cell, I saw Kilo at the small desk inside our cell, writing a letter.

"What's good, Lord?" I greeted him as I hung my coat on a hook on the wall.

"I ain't on shit. I'm writing shorty, telling her how she can get the tobacco to us. Plus, I'm breaking down the numbers she could see by fucking with us," Kilo said as he continued to pimp his pen.

I ain't gon' lie, my nigga had ambition when it came to accomplishing his goals. I just know Lord was a beast on the streets with the hustle, my kind of nigga.

"Gon' ahead and do you. I'm about to make something to eat. You trying to cook something, or you cool?" I asked him as I grabbed some items out of my locker.

"Nah, I'm cool, G. Appreciate it, though," he responded without even looking up from what he was doing.

Seeing I was riding solo on the meal, I grabbed my bowls and everything else I needed and left my cell on my way to the microwave. When I got to the microwave, I started to break the Ramen Noodles down, as eight new inmates came in the unit, escorted by two Correctional Officers, who held their name cards in their hands. There were five black inmates, one white boy, and two Hispanics. After the escorting officers gave the unit C.O. the name cards, they left. As soon as they did, three Soreno gang members approached the Hispanics and took them to a cell.

This was protocol for the Sorenos. They would take them to a cell and strip them naked and examine them for tattoos. They were looking for their enemies and if they found one, they were surely going to put the knife in his ass. I had just put my noodles in the microwave and started to cut up the summer sausage when I saw Kilo standing in front of our cell staring at me.

I waved my hand around the microwave as to say, *"Damn, my nigga—you can't see I'm cooking?"* His facial expression was too serious for me to keep standing there.

"Aye, my nigga, can you watch this real quick? When the soup is done go ahead and put your shit in. I'll be right back," I told this nigga named Woody from Baton Rogue, Louisiana, making my way back to my cell. When I walked, in Kilo was tying a shoestring around a shank that was hidden between the wall and the desk.

"What's good, Joe? What's wrong?" I asked as he got the six-inch pointed piece of steel ready to use.

"This nigga that just got off the bus name Mac-Glock, he was down in Victorville with me. This nigga was working with S.I.S and ended up telling one of y'all big homies named Doc about some cellphones. The folks crushed his ass, now he trying to get on Memphis time. The guys said that nigga had a greenlight on his head—that's on Chief!" Kilo said done prepping the weapon.

"A'ight, fam, but let me get that. You already know the folks handle their own work," I said and grabbed the shank from Kilo.

In all reality, I was going to use the situation to lay my gangsta down. To show these niggas around here what I was going to stand for and what I wasn't going to stand for—and rats, I wasn't going to stand for. Kilo left out of the cell and I followed him with the shank in front of my Russell Athletic jogging pants. When we approached Mac-Glock, he was standing at the bottom of the stairs with some Memphis dudes. He had a pillowcase slung over his right shoulder and his prison care package that the administration gives you before they release you to the compound. Mac-Glock was a light-skinned nigga with long dreads. He had on some prison-issued glasses. He was short and covered in tats.

"Damn, Kilo, what up homie?" The nigga Glock said to Kilo once we pulled up. He was smiling as if he was happy to see Kilo.

"Nigga you know what's up! Get your ass up outta here, you snitch ass nigga, before we fuck you around," Kilo said through clenched teeth. His arms folded over his broad chest.

"Come on man, Kilo. What type of shit you on?" Mac-Glock pleaded, wanting to talk about it.

I wasn't trying to rap, I pulled the knife out of my pocket. "Man, get the fuck up outta here pussy before you get crushed," I sneered.

Seeing that he was dealing with gangstas, Mac-Glock made a b-line to the officer's station. "C.O.—C.O., I gotta go, I can't be here!" Mac-Glock shouted to the correctional officer, letting him know that his life was now placed in danger.

The CO got on the walkie-talkie to get two C.O.s to escort Mac-Glock's scary-ass to the SHU, where the rodents were supposed to be. Knowing that the camera probably caught me upping the shank in the dayroom, I passed the shank to Swift G. Swift got the weapon, and went to hide it. That was my first time running somebody up as my adrenaline was now pumping. The look on Mac-Glock's face when I pulled the shank out, you woulda of thought I upped a Glock .40 with a thirty-shot extension, which boosted my morale!

An hour later, after we ran Mac Glock's hot ass up, they called the move for chow. Since I was the authority in the unit, I was to report all incidents, minor or major, and me running Glock up was considered major. So, I had to go to chow to let the guys know what had gone down. When me, Kilo, and Swift walked in the chow hall, I scanned around looking for Big Nasty or Hell-Boy. I didn't want to deal with neither one of them clowns, but since they were security I had to respect the authority of the chain of command.

As we made our way to the table, the only person with some authority that came to chow was one of the guys named G-Money. G-Money was from Rockford, Illinois, and was serving a life sentence for drugs. He had already served twenty-five years. G-Money was one of the guys, he was a laidback kind of dude, but he was on the unit with Big Nasty, so I knew he would give the business to him.

"Hey, what's going on with the men?" he asked with a smile as we sat down at the table.

"What's up, old head, you alright?" I said sitting next to him.

"Yeah, I'm a'ight. I'm thinking about quitting this kitchen job and getting a job working medical. Shit, a nigga trying to work around some bitches. This life sentence don't mean shit. I can put a hoe on the stroll, rain, sleet, or snow if she brings Daddy that doc."

"I see they can take the playa out the game, but they can't take the game out the playa," I told G-Money, shaking my head.

A lot of niggas would cry like a baby if they got sixty months, five years. But here it was, G-Money was serving a life sentence. His out date read deceased but yet he stayed in good spirits. He was the same person every day. I fucked with old head.

"Aye, G-Money, we just had an incident on the unit," I informed him.

His facial expression became serious. "What happened?" he inquired.

"One of the guys that got off the bus named Mac-Glock from Memphis. My celly says he was down in Victorville with him and he put S.I.S on doc about some phones. The guys crushed him and got him up outta there and greenlighted him. He came on the unit trying to get on Memphis time and we got him outta here," I told G-Money play-by-play.

"So, where he at now?" G-Money asked me.

"I just told you, G. We got him up outta here, he's in the SHU."

"Oh, oh, okay, that's the business youngsta. I'll let Big Nasty know when I get back on the unit. Other than that, y'all playas good?

"Yeah, we good. We just came out to report the incident, and if you run into Scrill tell 'em I said meet me at the library in the morning on the first move."

"I got you youngsta. Y'all just make sure you stay safe," G-Money replied.

I shook hands with G-Money the GD way and me, Kilo and Swift made our way back to the unit. When we got back in the unit a lot of niggas I had never spoken to was giving me head nods and what ups. Even KC, with his back-biting faggot ass had the nerve to speak. In prison, you had lions and you had sheep. The lions always ate and were respected through the jungle. The sheep are the ones that starved and only ate the scraps that were given. Lewisburg was the jungle, and I was a lion. The shit I was going through was making me show my teeth.

Tonight, was just the beginning. As the days were to come, I was going to roam the jungle as a predator—stealthy, stalking my prey. The rest of the night in Lewisburg Penitentiary was peaceful. I never got to make my food after getting locked in for the night. I had to settle for a bag of nacho chips. While banging my chips, I took time to use a razor blade to make one-book pieces of K-2. The clown ass nigga Lil Folks was giving me fifty books off this pack and I definitely needed it. But one thing for sure, when this lick came in with the C.O. bitch, me and Kilo's lives were going to change. We were going to feast around this bitch.

I finished cutting up the K-2 just as they turned out the lights, ending another night in captivity. After securing my pack on my body I hopped on the top bunk and pulled the sheet up to my neck. I was tired as hell, my thoughts were getting money and getting Lil Folks hot ass off the yard until I fell into a deep sleep.

The next morning the C.O. unlocked our cell door at 5:45 a.m. I was already awake and had been since 4:00 a.m., doing ab workouts. So, once the C.O. opened the door I was already dressed and ready to start my day. I quietly left the cell, careful not to wake

Kilo. I knew he wouldn't be getting up for another thirty minutes or so. I made my way to the computer to see if I had any emails. The feds were sweet. They gave us email access through Corrlinks, so we could stay in touch with our loved ones. It was better and faster than waiting for a letter through the regular mail.

After logging into my account, I saw that I had two emails. One from K.T. and one from this thick-ass white chick named Ashlie. She was from Virginia and was also in the feds doing time in Coleman, Florida. Shorty was doing fifteen years on a meth conspiracy. She was official and stood strong on her case. How we met is another story, but we had been talking for about three months. I read K.T.'s email first.

It read *It's done.*

I was geeked—excited as hell. It was on now, I couldn't wait to tell Kilo this shit. We were about to come the fuck up! I emailed him back and told him to send my love to Uncle Clyde and that I would be calling him soon. I then read Ashlie's email. Like all the rest of her emails, she sent me some freaky shit and said she couldn't wait to see me and hold me. I emailed her back some freaky, playa shit and logged off. Kilo was just walking out of the cell with a mean mug on his face.

My nigga definitely wasn't a morning person. He normally wouldn't start talking until about 9:30 am. This morning was going to be a different situation. Once I told him about what I just read in the email he wasn't going to be able to stop talking. I made my way over to the microwave where Kilo was warming up his coffee.

"Check it out, Lord, I just got off the email. My people said shorty handled that demonstration," I told him.

The nigga started smiling hard as hell. "It's on, Joe! We about to crush the yard!" he said as the microwave beeped, indicating his coffee was done.

Kilo took his coffee out of the microwave and suggested we go back to the cell. Lord had a pep in his step like he had just received clemency—a pardon on his sentence. Once we got in the cell he wasted no time.

"What did the email say, G? When that shit coming through?" This nigga was shooting questions like a Mac-11.

While Kilo was rambling about the riches we were about to obtain once the act landed, I hopped up to look out the window. It was raining and the clouds were dark, as lightning bolts struck through the sky. What piqued my interest was the GDs making their way across the yard. Walking toward my unit was Big Nasty, Hell-Boy, Chill, and two more of the guys, all a part of the security team.

"Aye, Kilo, check it out." Kilo came to the window and saw exactly what I saw.

"What's up with the folks? What they on?" he asked.

Just when I was about to respond a nigga named Reck from Detroit, Michigan called my name. I opened my cell door and peeked my head out the door. "What up?" I yelled.

"Aye, Lil Tony, Big Nasty at the door for you," Reck said nodding toward the front door.

I went to the door only to see Big Nasty standing there looking like a big gorilla with a skull cap on. His henchmen stood behind him looking like they were on some drama shit.

"What's good, G?" I asked from the other side of the door.

"What happened last night with that situation?" he inquired, his tone slightly aggressive.

"Oh, one of the guys got off the bus last night. My celly was at another spot with him and he said dude told on Doc about a cellphone. The guys put a greenlight on his head. The nigga came on the unit trying to get on Memphis time. So, I ran his rat ass up," I told Big Nasty.

"You ran him up? Who gave you authorization to run somebody up? Lil Folks got last say on who gets ran up on the yard, not you. Aye, come to the yard on the noon move," Big Nasty sneered, then turned on his heels and left with his cronies behind him.

"Shit!" I cursed out loud.

I went back to my cell to tell Kilo what had just transpired with these niggas. After telling him word for word what was said, the nigga looked at me and said, "Man, G, fuck them niggas. Dude hot as hell. Every GD in the system knows that nigga Mac-Glock is flaming. He gets crushed on every yard he lands on. How these niggas don't know that is crazy." Kilo didn't seem to be worried about the outcome of the situation. All he wanted to talk about was C.O. Jenkins and getting this pack in.

The whole day up until lunch I was a nervous wreck. I just knew these niggas were about to bring me a move. I had even gone to the library on the 8:30 move to get up with Scrill, but folks never showed up. It had been raining all day and if it stayed like this it was an eighty-five percent chance that Lil Folks, Big Nasty, and his goons wouldn't come out in the rain, but for those that don't know, my luck ain't shit. Twenty minutes before the move was called, the sun came out. It looked like the Simpsons was coming on, puffy white clouds and plenty of sunshine. I just couldn't win for losing.

Twenty minutes later the 12:30 move was called, and crowds of inmates descended from their units being released to the yard.

I slid my knife in the slit of my boxers for my own protection and made my way out of the unit to deal with the situation I had put myself in. Swift G came to the yard with me. He felt the same way I felt and to be honest he didn't like Lil Folks either. Walking over to the bench, I could see Lil Folks and the rest of the homies posted up. Lil Folks bore a mean mug on his face, but as I approached his mug turned into a smile.

"What's up, folks?" he greeted sticking his hand out.

"What's good, G?" I said as we shook hands the GD way.

"Ain't shit, let me rap with you real quick. Let's spin a lap," Lil Folks said, and we started to walk the track. We walked in silence for a couple of minutes until Lil Folks broke it, "You know S.I.S called me to the Lieutenant's office asking me about the nigga y'all ran up last night. They showed me a picture of dude asking me did I know him? I'm like I don't know this muthafucka. They said they saw you on camera brandishing a weapon. They said the only reason they didn't come look you up was because they wanted to see if I sanctioned his removal. But that's neither here nor there. You're not in the SHU, dude went up, so fuck 'em. But tell me what happened." Lil Folks walked with his hands clasped behind his back.

"Like I told G-Money and Big Nasty, my celly, Kilo was at USP Victorville with him. The nigga told on Doc about some cellphone shit. The guys crushed him, ran him up, and put a greenlight on him. When he got on the unit, he was trying to get on Memphis time. I figured it would be a security breach to leave him on the compound so—" I explained.

Lil Folks just nodded his head like he was agreeing with what I was speaking. "Lil Tony, what if fam you ran up had some dirt on Kilo and Kilo put the cables on you to get folks out of here before he got exposed? Not saying that's the case, but what if? G, you have to understand this Federal politicking can be deadly and vicious with it."

"How was I supposed to handle it?" I asked him, trying to see where he was going with this.

My celly was a good nigga, paperwork good, heart gold and lived by the G-code. That nigga couldn't have any dirt on Lord.

"It's three of y'all on the unit. Y'all supposed to put that nigga on GD arrest, follow him everywhere he go and give us time to investigate his allegations. Now, we can't do that because he's in the SHU. We could have put him on trial and if he came up guilty as charged, we coulda put a knife in him. Always remember Lil Tony, we seven-fours. It's a way we go about shit, always through low. It ain't what we do but how we do it. Don't trip, though, it ain't nothing but a learning experience. We all have them, G. Oh, on that package I gave you last night, you don't owe me nothing, we even," Lil Folks said.

I couldn't believe how this nigga was talking about law and all that shit. This rat was talking like he was standing on the business and was an official nigga. When he first got down here, he didn't want to be around none of the guys. Now he was speaking like he was chief—straight imposter! I wanted to pull my weapon and put it on him, but I knew now was not the time. I had to keep my emotions in check and play the game.

"I appreciate it family and I'm gonna learn from this situation. If this situation arises again, I will perform better believe that," I said.

"Nothing is wrong with making mistakes as long as we learn from them."

Me and Lil Folks continued to walk the yard fake kicking it until the 1:30 move was called, and we headed back to our assigned housing unit. When I came into the unit with Swift G I saw Kilo standing by the microwave looking like he was worried about something. I was about to go to the cell until I saw my window was covered. If kilo wasn't in the cell and the window was covered that meant only one thing, the C.O. was conducting a cell search.

"How long they been in there, Lord?" I asked Kilo as I walked up.

"Man, they been in there for about thirty minutes. It's C.O. Jenkins and that new fat white bitch Ms. Grails. They say Ms. Grails be booking niggas," Kilo informed me.

Twenty minutes later C.O. Jenkins and C.O. Grails came out of our cell and went to the officer station as me and Kilo made our way back. When we stepped into our severely small living quarters, it was as if we stepped into the aftermath of a tornado-like hurricane Katrina had hit. Our mattresses were flipped over. Pictures that were taped on the wall was ripped off and thrown on the floor, commissary items that were neatly put in the locker were now littering the floor. A box of washing powder was dumped in the middle of the floor. These folks had just fucked our shit up. I could see the steam coming off Kilo before he rushed out the cell, straight to the officer station.

"Kilo!" I yelled his name, trying to get him before he did something stupid.

I quickly checked between the desk and the wall, putting my hand between the desk. I felt the six-inch metal pick and I was relieved they didn't find the shank. Now, I had to go check and see how Kilo was handling the C.O. bitches. When I got to the officer's station where Kilo was, he was in the middle of cursing them out, calling them everything but a child of God.

"Stupid ass hoes! Call the Lieutenant! Y'all bogus as hell for disrespecting my property. I swear to God I'm writing you stupid bitches up!" My nigga vowed.

I just knew they were gonna hit the deuces and have compound officers come escort his ass to the SHU. Ms. Grails got off her fat ass, smiled, and then walked out of the office. C.O. Jenkins continued typing on the computer, without looking up at my fuming celly.

She asked, "Did you look in your pillowcase?"

"What?" he asked not hearing her correctly.

"I said—did you look in your pillowcase?"

Kilo caught the hint, then looked behind him and saw the whole dayroom was in his business, so he knew he had to put on a show.

"Stay the fuck out my cell you goofy ass bitch. I'm writing your dumb ass up," Kilo threatened loud as hell so everybody could hear him, faking like a muthafucka before he made his way back to the cell. When we got in the cell, I stood by the window on security while Kilo searched for what he was looking for. "She said the pillowcase, G? Where the fuck is it?" Kilo said.

"Look under the bunk, Lord," I told him.

Kilo did as I suggested. Moving the mattress out of the way he knelt and looked under the bed.

"I found it, G," he said, reaching under the bunk grabbing the brown pillowcase from underneath it.

When he dumped the pillowcase out, ten balled-up pairs of socks fell out. We both grabbed some socks and un-balled them. Plastic bags filled will tobacco fell from the socks.

"On chief, my nigga—we on!" Kilo yelled at the sight of the product.

"Man, pipe down fam. You loud as hell," I told Kilo trying to calm him down.

I can't lie, though, I was equally excited, but we had to keep shit on the low if we didn't want to end up in the SHU. We were in a United States penitentiary where the lions and savages roamed, but the fact of the matter was that it's still some mice around that had slipped through the cracks, and Lil Folks was one of them, so we had to be extra careful.

"Lil Tony, the bitch came through. I told you, my nigga!"

"Nigga, you ain't tell me shit! You were just out there blowing on the bitch, about to make her cry," I teased Kilo, looking back and forth from the cell window to all the tobacco that was on the table.

What we had was estimated to be a pound of tobacco in ten bundles. I mean, we didn't have a scale or anything, but we were both from the streets and could eyeball. After calming ourselves, me and Kilo cleaned up our cell and put everything back in order. We needed some plastic baggies, so I was going to get up with my nigga G-Money to see if he could get us some from the kitchen. I told Kilo it would be a good idea to stash the tobacco for about a week so nothing would look suspicious with the move that just got put down.

A lot of niggas in prison didn't have any business but to be in another nigga's business. Prison was nothing but one big house with everybody living under the same roof. A nigga watched you like an episode of *Love and HipHop*. Kilo agreed and we stashed the tobacco in our light cover we had made. We put it inside a sweatshirt before we put it in the light, to muffle the menthol smell. Kilo said when we bagged it up and sold it, we would bring back about ten grand profits, which was cool.

This was not just a trial run. C.O. Jenkins had compromised her job, she was now tied all the way in. Five stacks was a good start, but the ultimate goal was for her to bring that Dino in. Once she bought that Dino in, that's when we were gonna run that bag up—on the G!

Chapter 26

K.T.

Glancing at the face on the Bell and Ross time piece that surrounded my wrist. I noticed that this nigga Boo was running twenty minutes late. I was sitting in my Escalade in McDonald's parking lot on the Westside of Bloomington, waiting on Boo, so I could serve him this one-hundred grams of heroin. Boo was really starting to irk me. He had been driving back and forth from Chicago to cop work from me for the past six months. Instead of coming down here to get what he needed, the nigga was coming every other week grabbing the same one-hundred grams, which makes no sense. That was way too many transactions.

I kept telling him this, but he continued to keep moving the same way. I was taxing him a hunnid dollars a gram. The ten stacks he was bringing every other week was stacking up nice, so I continued to serve him. I met Boo at a strip club in Wisconsin Dells. We were at the bar and just happened to start talking. He commented on the Cartier watch I was rocking, and I admired the Sky-Dweller Rolex on his wrist. The nigga was definitely in the club dripping. The conversation went from jewelry to hoes to drugs.

Boo told me he was looking for a consistent plug on the Heroin. He said that the cat he was getting his work from was giving it to him for sixty-five dollars a gram, but his supplier wasn't consistent which was causing him to lose money. I told him my grams went for a hunnid but I was like a waterfall and never ran out. Boo said as long as he could cut the dope at least six times, he would be cool with paying a hunnid a gram. I assured him he could cut the dope at least eight times and it would still be a bomb. I stamped my product's potency because I was cutting it with fentanyl, but that information I held to myself.

Lil Tony had told me never to expose my hand. So, that's how I was moving. That was six months ago and since then, I had grossed about one-hundred and twenty bands. It's good money, but if this nigga didn't tighten up on how he was moving, I was going to have to cut his water off. Ten minutes later Boo swerved into the parking lot in a smoke grey Challenger and parked on the side of my Cadillac truck. I looked over to see some dark-skinned cat with dreads in the passenger seat. This nigga Boo was gonna make me do something to his ass, straight up! He knew not to bring nobody with him when he came to meet me on some business. He was tripping.

I watched as Boo hopped his skinny, lanky ass out of his whip. He was a light-skinned nigga with 360 waves. He was about 6'1 and wore a lot of loud jewelry. I was starting to look at Boo like he was a straight clown. I was steaming as Boo got in the passenger seat of the lac truck.

"What it do, gym shoe?" he asked closing the door.

"Who the fuck is that?" I said, then looked over at the dude sitting in Boo's whip.

I mean mugged him, letting him know I didn't approve of his presence. The nigga just turned his head trying to avoid contact, then I turned my attention back to Boo.

"Be cool, family. That's my man's off my block. I'm dropping him off in Peoria before I head back to the city," Boo replied.

"My nigga, you couldn't do that shit after we handled this business?" I asked the dumb nigga.

"I just figured it wouldn't be that big of a deal," Boo weakly said as he handed me the purple Crown Royal bag containing the ten thousand.

I nodded my head toward the cupholder that held a McDonald's cup, the one-hundred grams of dope inside of it. "Another thing, we're done with this every other week shit. You either come once a month and get what you gon' get or we gon' have to conclude our business, period," I told him. This time I was going to stand on what I was speaking.

Boo nodded his head before he said, "I got you big dog. I'm just trying to get my weight up like you, my nigga! I see you shining, my dude. Big Boy, Bell, and Ross on the wrist. I know that costs you about fifty. How do I get on your level?" he said cheesing.

"Aye, fam, check it out, you cool? I got some shit to do," I asked Boo, ready for him to get the fuck out of my truck.

It wasn't so much I didn't trust Boo. It was the nigga sitting in the passenger seat. Dude rubbed me the wrong way. I was trying to get the fuck away from his ass. Boo gave me some dap and said he would get up with me next month on the re-ups. When he did, he was going to double his load and got out of the truck. I looked over at the nigga with the dreads once more. The nigga had a smirk on his face, and it was at this moment I had a gut feeling something was definitely up with fuck boy.

After pulling out of the McDonald's parking lot, I got en-route back to the crib. A lot of shit was going on in my life. My cousin Lil Tony had some correctional officer call my phone saying I was to Western Union her five thousand dollars. Lil Tony had already put me up on the play, so after she gave me the information I needed, I went to the nearest Western Union and wired the five gees. Whoever shorty was, she said she would be keeping in touch. I don't know what my cousin was on but I knew it was some federal shit. I just hope he knew what he was doing. That was my nigga, my blood, so I was rocking with him to the fullest.

Then two weeks ago Tiff told me that she missed her period. After taking a pregnancy test, it came back positive. I was about to be a father. I was happy as hell, so was Tiff. We had been trying to have a child, and now Allah had just blessed us. Knowing we had a baby on the way, Tiff wanted me to slow down on the street hustling and get into some legal shit. I wanted to do just that, but I didn't have the slightest clue as to what I wanted to do. I'm from the projects in Chicago, all I knew was the streets.

I definitely had to figure some shit out, and soon. Pulling up in my driveway, I saw Kevin's cherry red Durango. I was glad he was at my crib. I had heard through the streets that Kevin's white ass was going around slanging that steel full throttle. I hadn't seen him since I had him park Heath's ass a few weeks ago. Kevin was a quiet dude, but he stayed in some shit if that makes any sense. I learned that Kevin was beefing with a few different cliques throughout the city. He was sliding to Chicago knocking niggas down. Come to find out, most of Kevin's beef was over social media shit.

Tiff even told me that her nephew was on Instagram posing with twin Dracos. Shorty was starting to do a lot of dumb shit that could get him under a Federal Penitentiary. He was my shooter, so I needed him out here on the streets with me. I grabbed the Crown Royal bag out of the glove compartment and got out of the truck. Walking inside my crib I was greeted by the smell of high-grade marijuana.

Kevin was in the living room, tapping on the PlayStation controller, playing 2K-20. A blunt was dangling between his lips and a Glock with a 30-round magazine laid at his feet, between his legs. He looked up at me, nodded his head in acknowledgment, took a strong pull from the backwood, and held it out to me. I tossed the Crown Royal bag with the ten racks in it on the sectional sofa and accepted the blunt from him.

"Where Tiff at?" I asked while I filled my lungs with the exotic strain.

"She's upstairs," Kevin replied blowing out smoke.

I continued smoking the weed. The THC went through my bloodstream immediately, getting me to where I needed to be. After another pull, I passed the blunt back to Kevin.

"Where the hell you been Macaulay Culkin? I ain't seen you in about three weeks," I said looking over at Kevin.

Shorty was fresh to death, rocking a red and black Fendi sweat suit. He was a white boy with swag.

"Just been trying to lay low. Trying to stay out of these niggas way, that's all," he replied high as hell.

"I don't see how you trying to stay low posting choppas on Instagram and shit," I said.

He looked at me through his red eyes. "Gotta let these niggas know what they facing if they jump out there. If they know how I'm coming, maybe they'll stay in their lane and know this ain't what they want," Kevin retorted.

"Or put the feds on you and get you sent to Lewisburg where my cousin Lil Tony at. You got to use your head, Kevin. The feds all on that Facebook shit. You can't even fight that in court," I said trying to get Kevin to see the consequences of his reckless behavior.

He was just like the rest of the young cats out here, gone off designer drugs and Drill Music. Kevin had a rough life growing up. At three years old he was put in a foster home, that he often ran away from as he got older. He went from foster home to foster home, then graduated to Juvenile facilities to County Jails. The more time Kevin served in jail the worse he came out. Being housed with so many gangsters and criminals, Kevin had no choice but to adapt to the criminal element.

Having a deadbeat father and a crack-addicted mother who was Tiff's sister. The only love Kevin got was from his peers in the streets. Going through so much in his life made him become emotionally dysfunctional, as well as violent. His love for guns and quick prone to violence was the mix that made him into the terrorist that he is today. Kevin used his violent tactics in the streets to suppress his issues. I knew his heartless attitude would be beneficial to what I was trying to achieve, so I wanted him by my side. Plus, he was family. I just needed him to move smarter than how he was moving.

"Aye, Kevin, my nigga, you ain't got nothing to prove to these niggas. Gangsta's don't Facebook shit. You only putting yourself out there to the world—putting muthafuckas in your business. You already know if a nigga gets wrong and it got to get like that, lay on your man then hit your man. I already got one person I love behind the wall. I don't need another one. You feel me?"

Kevin put the game on pause before he turned back to look at me. "K.T., I love you too, fam and on the strength of you, I'm gon' chill out. You been nothing but a real brother to me since you came around and I appreciate it. That ten stacks you gave me for busting dude shit, I invested six of it. My man gave me three pounds of cookies for six racks. That's what we smoking on now. I'ma fall back on these niggas and start getting to some money. Until you call me to come through to drop something," Kevin said speaking from the heart.

I smiled at him starting to see the bigger picture. The money.

"That's what I'm talking about, nephew. So, you hustling loud now, huh?"

"Yeah, something like that," Kevin replied, then un-paused the game.

"Two stacks a pound is a lil steep, don't you think?" I asked pertaining to the prices he was paying.

"Not really. If I sell one-hundred-dollar quarters. That's seven hundred off an ounce, sixteen ounces in the pound. I'ma make sixty-four hundred dollars minus the two grand I spent. I come off with forty-four hundred profit, not bad," Kevin said breaking down his hustle.

"That's cool if you trying to be on some lil nigga shit. It's fifteen-year old's out here hustling on that level. I tell you what, holla at your peeps and tell 'em you got one-hundred racks to spend. See what you can get for that. If the numbers right, we gon' grab it. If not, I got somebody else in mind. I want you to wholesale, get your bag all the way up. We ain't playing with these niggas, fam. We gon' stand as giants over these midgets out here," I told him.

I was a major figure in these streets. Ain't no way I was gonna have my people out here hustling on some lil boy shit! After smoking two more blunts and beating Kevin's ass on 2K-20, I made my way upstairs to see what was up with Tiff. Walking in our master bedroom, I saw my Queen peacefully sleeping in our king-size canopy bed. I quietly went into our walk-in closet where I had our safe built in the wall. Opening it I put the ten stacks in, adding it to the seven hundred thousand that was stacked neatly inside. After I put my paper up, I went over to the bed and stared at Tiff as she slept.

My wifey was beautiful. I loved her and knowing she was carrying my seed in her womb made me love her even more. I stood there wondering what we would have, a boy or a girl. In all reality, it didn't even matter, as long as our child was healthy, and it came from Tiff I would be blessed. I was three hundred gees away from a million. I had to find something to invest this money in, something that would be held at value if anything happened to me. Something Tiff and our child could fall back on. Maybe some real estate or a store or some shit. One thing about it, once I got that mill, I was getting out of the game.

Chapter 27

Kilo

It had been two weeks since C.O. Jenkins dropped off the sac to us. Me and my celly bust that shit down and got to business. The breakdown was more profitable than we thought it would be. We were able to bag up to thirteen pouches. It was six cups in a pouch and a cap cost ten books of stamps which was seventy-five dollars in penitentiary money. Off six caps, which was a pouch, we would make four hundred and fifty dollars and we had thirteen pouches netting us five thousand, eight hundred and fifty dollars.

We ended up giving Swift G six cups on consignment for five books a cap, giving him some room to maneuver. He was on the unit with us so it was a must he ate with us. I fucked with Swift G. He was a solid nigga. I was going to give K.D. some tobacco to hustle but Lord was in the SHU. Supposedly, he had smoked some K-2 and had an episode. They say the nigga bust out his cell with just his boxers on, sweating and swinging his knife in the air, screaming that demons were trying to kill him. One of the Lords who went by the name of Seville had already sent word to our big homie. When the email came back that K.D. was to be removed from his position, Seville was to oversee the Vice Lords at Lewisburg.

I talked to the Captain and asked were they going to let K.D. back on the yard and he said K.D. was getting out of the SHU in ninety days. I was glad my nigga was not getting transferred because of that bullshit. K.D. was my nigga, I didn't judge Lord because he smoked K-2. Hell, I had even smoked it a few times. I just wanted K.D. to get out of the SHU and get his mind right. He had a lot of potential and a solid reputation in the feds, but I was always taught it took years to get a solid reputation and only a second to destroy it.

Plus, Lord was about to go home in three years, so he had to get his mind right before his release or the cold world would swallow him whole. The tobacco was moving fast as hell on the yard. We had so many books of stamps we had to stash them in other niggas cells. With all the money we were getting, you already know the thirsty niggas was on the lurk. I was on the yard a few days ago when I was approached by the GDs, Lil Folks, Big Nasty, and Hell-Boy.

They pulled up on me asking me about an incident I had with a Louisiana nigga named N.O. Me and the nigga N.O. had some words over some stamps. He was a bully-type nigga who tried to use his size and press game on me but found out quick that I wasn't going. I sold this nigga a square for a book of stamps right before 9:30 count lockdown. The next night, yeah you heard right, the next night N.O. pulled up on me talking about I sold him some fake tobacco and he wanted his book of stamps back. I looked at his George Foreman looking ass like he was crazy.

"N.O., come on, fam. I sold you the same tobacco I've been selling everybody else. You're the only one complaining," I told him.

"That shit fake round, it keeps going out. My celly said it's some Indian tobacco," N.O. said in his Louisiana drawl.

"Indian tobacco? Fam, I did straight business with you. I don't know what you on, but what's up? What you want from me? I'm about to go hop on this phone," I said trying to figure out where he was going with the bullshit.

"What I want is my book of stamps back," he had the nerve to say through clenched teeth like he was intimidating somebody.

I smiled at him. "Hold that thought, nigga," I said and walked off from him.

My destination—my cell. When I got to my cell, I grabbed my knife from the stash, wrapped a shoestring around the bottom of it to use as a handle, put it in my pocket, and left-back out of the cell. N.O. was still standing in the same spot like the big dummy that he was when I walked back up with my hands in my pockets.

"N.O., I'm not giving you nothing. So where do we go from here?" I said, my tone calm, yet deadly as I looked him in the eyes.

A lot of dudes had seen the situation, as all eyes were on us. These niggas were expecting bloodshed. Six of N.O.'s Louisiana homeboys noticed what was going on and came over to see what the business was. At the same time, Lil Tony and Swift G pulled up ready to Aid and Assist me. We were outnumbered easily on the unit, but one thing about it, we were on gang time and we were trained to go win, lose or draw.

"Aye N.O., what's going on 'round?" Woody asked.

Woody was from Baton Rouge, Louisiana. He was a young playa. Even though he was young at only twenty-five years of age, Woody was more mature than most of his older homies.

"Dude sold me some fake tobacco for a book, and I want my book of stamps back," This stupid ass nigga said.

Woody looked at me. I peeped one of their homies lacing up his sneakers.

"I don't owe N.O. shit, Woody. This nigga bought a square from me last night. Now he's talking about it was fake and he wants his stamps back. I don't know what kind of depo-fiend shit N.O. on, but I ain't going. Not even at gun point," I stated standing my ground.

On Vice Lord, I wasn't going for nothing. These niggas were gonna have to kill me before I went out like a bitch…on the fam! Woody turned his attention back to N.O.

"You bought a square last night and you just now saying something about it?" Woody asked him.

"Uh-huh," N.O. responded, looking like the slow nigga from the Green Mile.

"Where the fake cigarette N.O.?" Woody asked getting irritated with his homie.

"I smoked it," the dummy said looking stupid as hell when he said it.

Woody looked like he wanted to slap the shit out of him. "N.O., get the fuck away from me before your ass be in the SHU round and this situation is over with. Kilo don't owe you shit. Get the fuck away from me," Woody sneered.

N.O. walked off with his head down, looking like a dinosaur with his goofy ass.

"You good, Kilo?" Woody asked, extending his hand, which I accepted.

"Yeah, I'm good, bro. You already know how N.O. be on his bullshit," I told Woody letting him know I didn't hold any ill-feeling towards N.O.

"Well, round better get his shit together before his ass be in the SHU with some puncture wounds. We trying to keep it peaceful around here, especially with the real niggas," Woody said.

We shook hands putting the whole incident to rest. That was the extent of it. How Lil Folks found out about it, I don't know. But they definitely pulled up on me about it. I told the folks the incident as it happened, and I guess they used that as an outlet to get in on what me and Lil Tony had going on.

"Damn, Lord, you willing to blow the yard with Louisiana over a four-dollar book of stamps? You already know we're in a coalition and if the Vice Lords get into it then the folks have to Aid and Assist," Lil Folks said like I was new in the system.

"I know this, so what you saying?" I said. This nigga was beating around the bush.

"I'm just saying, Lord, you around here with the plug on the squares. The guys trying to eat. We ain't asking for no handouts. We trying to spend some money with you. What will you do if we come up with five-hundred dollars?" He probed.

Lil Folks couldn't know how we were getting it. It was only me and Lil Tony a part of the move and I know he wasn't going to tell nobody shit. Me and fam had already discussed what we would say when these niggas came around on some bullshit, exactly what I was about to tell Lil Folks hot ass.

"Man, bro, I ain't got it like that. A nigga blessed my hand with a few caps and he charging the shit out of me. But what I can do is see what he would do for the five hundred. I'm just the middleman," I said spinning Lil Folks like a CD.

Lil Folks looked at me like he was pondering what I was saying, trying to decipher if I was telling the truth.

"Alright, fam, just keep me posted," he replied before he spent off with his henchmen following behind him like the flunkies that they were. I knew Lil Folks was just fishing for information. I wasn't gonna fuck with that nigga if he had $50,000 to spend. Dude was a rat and that got some good niggas life in prison. I wasn't fucking with him—period!

After Lil Folks moved around, I continued to walk the track. Looking over at the bench, I saw the guys over there kicking it. My homie Crazy Lord from Grand Rapids, MI was over there entertaining the guys as usual. I was on my way over until this white boy named Zimmer approached me to get some cigarettes. Zimmer always spent a lot of money so I would give him plays. Zimmer was a rapper from South Dakota who went by the name of Ape Shit.

I had even seen one of his videos on MTV a few times when I was in the free world. He had a song with Wacka Flacka called "I Ain't Know" that was tight as hell. Zimmer threw his career away when he got out of State Prison and O.J. Simpson'd his wife and her lover. Now he's serving a life sentence in the feds, but me and Zimmer were cool.

"Aye, Kilo, what's up, man?"

"Ain't nothing. What up, white boy?"

"You still got squares?"

"You already know," I responded, scanning my surroundings to make sure nobody was in my business.

I saw my celly and Scrill standing by the hardball court, incognito. Me and Lil Tony caught eye contact. He smiled at me and gave me the thumbs up. What that was about, I didn't know, but I was surely going to find out.

"I got seven books, Kilo, fuck with me," Zimmer said pulling out a knot of stamps.

I looked around once more before I went in my pants to get the plastic baggie with the squares in it.

"I got you, Joe," I said and went in the baggies to get his tobacco.

It was folded tightly in pieces of paper. Each paper held enough tobacco to roll one jailhouse cigarette. I gave Zimmer ten of them for his seven books of stamps.

"Good looking, Kilo. Aye, my homie got some shine coming down later tonight. Pull up on me later and I'ma bless your game," Zimmer said as he hid the squares on his body.

"Best believe I'm a slide on you," I replied.

Not going to miss out on some good ole jailhouse Ciroc. The white boys made the best liquor in prison. I put the stamps in my pocket and made my way over to the bench to kick it with the guys. I had only been on the yard for an hour and already made sixty books—two hundred dollars. A lot of niggas were starting to hate, but this wasn't shit. We were about to give they're ass something to hate on for real. Making my way over to the bench, I looked over at Lil Tony and Scrill again. They were on something heavy. Little did I know, a lot of shit was about to get exposed and when it did, it was about to go down around this bitch.

Chapter 28

Lil Tony

"This ho ass nigga!" I told Scrill, as we went over Lil Folks' paperwork pertaining to his indictment.

Black Mac and Stackhouse had sent word out about Lil Folks being a rat. But to read it myself was a whole different beast. Not only did he tell on his co-defendants on his case, but this nigga got some more time while serving his sentence. Apparently, he was at Fort Dix, a medium-security facility, when this clown tried to have his own mama bring him a couple of ounces of meth into the prison.

They were monitoring his phone call and his dumbass was reckless with his language. They bumped his moms at the door. She allowed them to search her, and the drugs were found. Both Lil Folks and his mother were indicted on possession of methamphetamine and bringing drugs on the grounds of a federal correctional facility. Since Lil Folks had high criminal history points he was facing a minimum of twenty years to life on the indictment. He decided to cooperate—again. He snitched on his mama and the dealer that had given her the drugs.

They ended up giving his mama six years and the dude who gave her the work eight years in federal prison. Lil Folks ended up getting one-hundred and eighty-eight months, fifteen years ran concurrent to his three-hundred, sixty-month sentence. So basically, he didn't get no time. This nigga was the crudest dude I had ever crossed paths with. We also got the email to Big Cliff so we could verify the email Lil Folks said that he sent him saying he was to oversee the yard. Big Cliff said he didn't even know who Lil Folks was and never heard of him. He also said he knew nothing of the incident with Black Mac and Stackhouse and we should do everything in our power to get them both out of the SHU and back on the yard.

As far as Lil Folks, we were to do what needed to be done. Me and Scrill both knew what that meant. We had to get Lil Folks off the yard, and he couldn't walk up. We had to punish him and that was the business. Since Lil Folks had most of the guys subordinate and loyal to his leadership, we would have to be very strategic with this. The guys were following Lil Folks only because he was feeding them K-2, keeping them high and with a few stamps in their pockets. That is what me and Scrill were on the yard discussing at this moment, his removal.

"I say we call an Open Discussion and show the guys this nigga paperwork and this email from Big Cliff. That's the right way to do it," I told Scrill, ready to handle this Nation business. I was tired of even looking at Lil Folks hot ass.

"How many of the guys you really think care about Lil Folks being hot or that email from Big Cliff? He's feeding them G. It's just how it is on the streets. Niggas ain't following the G-code. They're following the nigga with the bag. It's the same way in here, fam. All this shit is starting to get watered down to a point. It's only a few good men like us that's really standing on this Nation business.

"All the other men are focused on following behind the niggas that are giving them handouts. Look at Big Nasty, he supposed to be the backbone of the membership and he let Lil Folks take the yard. What happened don't take a rocket scientist to figure it out. Him being security, he was supposed to investigate that email and find out if it was official. Instead of allowing Lil Folks to step up in that position, then turn around and run Stackhouse up for no reason, only shows his insubordination to the laws and politics that govern us."

"That's why he should be the first to go, then Lil Folks," I said cutting Scrill off.

Big Nasty was the threat. Lil Folks was nothing without Big Nasty. Lil Folks was only the dictator. If he had nobody to dictate he was nothing. Big Nasty was his send-off. Us getting Big Nasty off the yard was equivalent to disarming Lil Folks. Scrill nodded his head in understanding like he saw the merit in what I was saying.

"You make sense, Lil Tony, but who we gon' get to get Big Nasty off the yard? And how we gon' do it? I mean, whoever does it is definitely going to have to go to the SHU and whoever we get to do it is gon' have to be trustworthy enough not to alert him of our intentions. If this happens, then you already know how this is gon' play out," Scrill said.

What he spoke definitely made sense. We had to come up with a way to get Big Nasty off the compound quietly but efficiently. I quickly came up with a plan to bring this nigga a move of violence.

"Since folks always looking for a handout, we gon' rock his ass all the way to sleep. He already knows we're fucking with the tobacco. We're gonna tell him we gon' put him on so he can make some money. But he gotta come on the unit to get his pack. When he gets to the unit, we gon' crush his ass. It's a nigga in my unit named Jazzy from the Eastside of Detroit, big young nigga. I've seen shorty knock a few niggas out on the unit. Shorty with all the shits.

"I say we pay him to get on Big Nasty, have him put the lock on him. Then once we get Big Nasty gone, we call a meeting with the guys, present the email and his paperwork, and before he says anything I'ma blast his ass and run him up. And, if any of the other guys want to Aid and Assist him I guess we just gon' have to blow the yard. That's a sacrifice I'm willing to make at this point," I said.

"I feel you, family. It sounds like a plan. After we remove this rodent then what?" Scrill asked.

Then we holla at S.I.S and see if we can get Black Mac and Stackhouse out of the SHU. They're only back there because of Lil Folks police ass. Once they see the GDs are the ones that got him off the yard, they gon' figure it was an executive decision to remove him. They gon' know it was a call from the higher up. Come on, Scrill, you been doing this fed shit longer than me. You know this, G."

How you know shorty from Detroit gon' be with the move? His car might not approve of his actions. You know they can't get in on gang business," Scrill questioned.

"I know shorty gon' be with it because shorty about that money. We come with a stack, Jazzy gon' crush that nigga. As far as his Detroit homies, Jazzy don't respect their authority. He already thinks he's the King of Detroit anyway. The young nigga is rebellious as shit. He be on the unit robbing niggas and all types of shit. Plus, he fucks with me hard. For a band, he'll bust Big Nasty's head to the white meat. I'ma holla at Jazzy when I get back on the unit and I'ma let you know the demonstration at breakfast in the morning," I told Scrill, letting him know I was on top of this shit. I was pushing the gas on full throttle. I was trying to get these clowns gone like yesterday.

"I'm with you, fam. Let's get these imposters gone. Make sure you're at breakfast in the a.m. so we can go over details," Scrill said as we shook hands the GD way.

I saw my celly walking the track with Lil Folks and Big Nasty. We caught eye contact, I smiled and gave him the thumbs up. He looked at me with confusion. I knew he didn't know what the thumbs up was for, but I was definitely going to bring him into the fold once we got back in the cell.

I continued to walk the track and politic with my folks Scrill. until they called the move for us to go back to our housing unit. I noticed Lil Folks and Big Nasty ducked off in the cut watching our every move. Little did they know the lines had been drawn in the sand. We now had our orders from Big Cliff to handle this Nation business. Lil Folks had deceived the membership by presenting a bogus email and lying on a board member, and he did it all to gain a position of power. Being subordinate to the body and adhering to the chain of command, we were going to make sure Lil Folks paid for his disloyalty—and he was going to pay in blood.

When I came back in the unit, my first order of business was to find Jazzy. I looked around the unit and couldn't find shorty. I saw his homeboy Reck, at the computer checking his emails. Reck stayed on the computer. He was getting to a bag in Detroit, so he had a gang of bitches emailing him. Reck was a playa.

"Reck, what's good, Joe? Where's Jazzy?" I asked as I approached him.

"He should be in Woody's cell shooting dice," Reck said, not even looking up from the computer as he typed.

"Alright, good looking thug," I said and made my way to Woody's cell.

When I got to his cell, I looked through the cell window and saw at least seven niggas in the small cell gambling. I tapped on the door before I entered. As I came in the cell I saw that Jazzy was shaking the dice. He looked up at me before he rolled the dice.

"Oh, shit, my broke ass old head just came in the room. Y'all know I'm 'bout to hit this point. I need these stamps to get my old-head a new jogging suit!" he joked before the dice left his hand.

Ten books in stamps were in the pot as one of the dice continued to spin, one dice was already showing a one. Jazzy had a 6-8 bet going on for ten books. The spinning dice landed on 6, thus making the dice read 7. Jazzy had just crapped out—losing. Three different dudes reached in the pot getting their share of the ten books.

"Jazzy, sweet as honey," a dude named Sed said, grabbing his stamps off the floor.

"Sweet? Bitch ass nigga say that shit again. I'll slap the shit out of your soft ass and take them pussy ass stamps," Jazzy threatened.

"Man, Jazzy, you tripping," Sed pleaded, knowing Jazzy would make good on his threat.

"Nah, nigga, you tripping. That's why niggas be getting poked up around this bitch, because niggas don't know how to watch what come out they fucking mouths," Jazzy sneered.

I laughed at him. I knew Jazzy was just on his Jazzy bullshit.

"Aye, Jazzy, when you finished gambling come holla at me. I got a lick for you," I told him before I walked out the cell.

"A lick? Shit, I'm done right now old head. I need to get up outta here anyway before I have to fuck one of these niggas up," Jazzy said following me out the cell, mean-mugging Sed as he walked past him.

"What up doe, Lil Tony?" Jazzy asked me once we were out of Woody's cell.

"Meet me in my cell in about five minutes, bro," I said.

"Alright, that's a bet," he responded.

I went by my cell and went in my stash. I grabbed ten bundles of stamps, ten books in each bundle equaling one hundred books—one thousand dollars in compound money. I put the stamps in my front pocket. A few minutes later Jazzy was knocking at my cell door. I waved for him to come on in, which he did.

"What up, doe?" he said closing the cell door behind him.

"You trying to make some money, young nigga?" I asked.

"What kind of question is that? What I gotta do?"

"I need you to bust a nigga's head."

"Who?"

"One of my homies," I replied.

"What's the ticket?" Jazzy inquired.

I pulled the bags of stamps out of my pocket and tossed it to him. He caught it mid-air.

"How many books is this?" he asked, eyes big as hell.

"That's a hunnid books, my nigga—a thousand dollas."

"Shiiid—where the nigga at? He on the unit?" Jazzy was ready to get active.

"Pump your brakes, fam. We gotta do this shit a certain way. For the one hunnid books you gon' have to put that pad-lock on his ass. I want this nigga's shit to be swollen like a pumpkin."

"For a hunnid books, I'll put that knife in his ass. That's on my mama!" Jazzy said all the way turnt up.

"Nah, just put the lock on him. We gon' have him on the unit tomorrow. When they call the move and he about to leave to go back to his unit, get on his ass but you gotta crush him bad, Jazzy. You gon' have to go to the SHU, but on my word, as my word is my bond, we gon' get you out. I'ma give you three caps of tobacco to hustle while you back there in the SHU so you can continue to make money."

"Man, for a stack and three caps I'ma make sure they air lift his ass. Matter of fact, who is it?" Jazzy asked wanting to know the identity of his victim.

I was reluctant to give Jazzy this information, but since he was the one putting in the work, I had more respect for him. I had to tell him. If Big Nasty showed up on the unit and Jazzy saw it was Big Nasty and reneged on the contract things could go left. But at the same time, if I revealed who it was, and Jazzy informed Big Nasty shit could still go left. You never know what kind of relationships niggas held with each other. At this point, it was about taking a chance. We had to get these suckas off the yard.

"Big Nasty—one of my GD homies," I told Jazzy. Jazzy put the bag of stamps in his pocket.

"Big Nasty, huh? Well, Big Nasty ass about to get smoked. I don't like his ass anyway. I would have done that shit for free."

"Well, give me them books back since you'll do it for free."

"Nah, I'ma keep 'em," Jazzy said making his way out the cell.

"I know broke ass nigga, stop with all that capping," I joked as he left the cell.

While Jazzy was on his way out, Kilo was on his way in.

"What up, Joe? What's up with Jazzy's wild ass? They say he just got punished on the dice fucking with Woody and them," Kilo said plopping down on his bunk.

"Man, fuck that! Wait till you hear this shit." I said and started to roll a cigarette.

After putting the finishing touches in the square, I lit it using the two double-A batteries and a thin piece of wire. Taking a strong pull from the menthol tobacco, I exhaled the smoke through my nostrils as I filled Kilo in on the latest events of the day. I told him about how we finally got Lil Folks legal documents and that Lil Folks was a certified stamped rat that even testified on his own mother. I also let him know how Scrill got Big Cliff's email and how we emailed Big Cliff trying to verify the email that was supposed to have come from him, saying Lil Folks was the chosen overseer for the GDs.

Big Cliff said he didn't know who Lil Folks was and to handle him swiftly. I also informed Kilo about how I paid Jazzy to hit Big Nasty tomorrow and that I was going to stab Lil Folks and run him up in front of the guys. The plan was simple. I was going to pull up on Big Nasty tomorrow and tell him to come to my unit and we were gonna give him some caps to hustle. When he came on the unit Jazzy was gon' paint the dayroom with his blood. I also told Kilo that I had just given Jazzy one hunnid books for the hit. Kilo tilted his head back with a confused look.

"A hunnid books! Fam, you could have gave a random nigga a piece of K-2 to do that shit! A thousand dollas—bro you tripping!" Kilo said.

"A stack ain't shit. That stack gon' make sure shit gets done right—trust me," I replied.

The contract on Big Nasty had already been taken. Now all I needed was for Jazzy to put that work in and I was going to take care of everything else.

Me and Kilo continued to rap about what was to transpire the next day. Kilo also wanted to go over some numbers with me as far as our hustle. We had already made over $3,500 minus the stack I just gave Jazzy. We were blowing through this shit. He had even told me he talked to C.O. Jenkins about making the next move. I had to get up with K.T. asap and give him the heads up so that when C.O. Jenkins called about that dope, lil cuz would already be on point. That's why we had to hurry up and get this politicking shit over with so we could get to this money.

Chapter 29

The next morning Lil Tony and Scrill sat in the chow hall politicking Big Nasty's removal, as well as Lil Folks demise over a bowl of corn flakes and a danish. Today would be the day the insubordinate acts of Lil Folks would be exposed to the membership. It would be a strong possibility that after today's events, the Lewisburg Penitentiary would be placed on lockdown status due to the violence that was about to take place in the prison. Scrill brought up the fact that he felt Hell-Boy should leave as well since he was Big Nasty's assistant and followed behind him. Lil Tony had a difference in opinion. Lil Tony felt that Hell-Boy had good potential and was just misled.

"Fam, if we leave Hell-Boy on the yard who's to say he won't go around trying to cause disconnection amongst the men? Then we gon' be right back to where we started," Scrill stated. He didn't trust Hell-Boy and wanted him gone.

"Bro, Hell-Boy is a shorty. He from South Carolina, but what structure is he following? Down there they just running around calling themselves self Gs. A lot of them don't even know their history, how we transitioned from Gangster Disciples to Growth and Development. They don't get their intellect until they come to prison. Until then, they just be out there on some shit. I was the same way. Lil Folks brainwashed Hell-Boy to be on some bullshit like he did with a lot of the other guys. But I guarantee you, once they see the consequences for going against the grain, they gon' see how real this shit is. Watch what I tell you," Lil Tony said, taking a bite out of his danish.

"Okay, Lil Tony, I'ma leave it in your hands. You know if we leave folks on the yard and he gets on some other shit, and one of the guys get hurt, it's gon' fall in your lap?" Scrill asked Lil Tony with a raised eyebrow, wanting him to see the seriousness of the call he was about to make.

"I'm already hip, G. If Hell-Boy jumps out there after today I'ma poke his ass up myself and get him off the yard."

"Or—you gon' be the one getting poked up," Scrill said nonchalantly as he ate his cereal.

"Yeah, I know the business, fam, more words need not be explained."

Lil Tony knew that by vouching for Hell-Boy he was taking a deadly chance, but he felt in his heart Hell-Boy was truly one of the brothers. He just needed to be around some righteous individuals to groom him the right way. He had twenty-five years to do in the concrete jungle and he had just started his bid. He was going to have to be around the right caliber of niggas and learn from them if he wanted to have a chance of making it out of the feds alive, or without catching another case. Lil Tony didn't feel like Scrill had to throw a threat of violence in the air. That rubbed him the wrong way.

Lil Tony stored the threat in his mental Rolodex and would never forget the words that rolled off Scrill's tongue, *Or, you can be the one getting poked up.* Keeping his emotions in check, Lil Tony and Scrill rapped about the day's events until they had to leave the chow hall and head back to their units. When they stepped outside, they stood posted for a couple of minutes.

"Make sure you tell Big Nasty to meet me on the yard on the 12:30 recreation move. Tell 'em it's Nation business," Lil Tony told Scrill.

"Don't even trip, family, I'ma make sure he gets the message. You just make sure you're on the yard to meet him—and Lil Tony?"

"What up, G?"

"Keep this shit to yourself," Scrill warned.

"You already know, silence and secrecy," Lil Tony retorted and shook hands with Scrill the GD way before they made their departure, in their own thoughts, motivated to stand on this Nation business.

Later, that day, after the afternoon lunch, the 12:30 recreation move was called. Lil Tony made his way to the yard. Walking on the yard he spotted Big Nasty, Hell-Boy, and a few of the Vice Lords posted on the bench shooting the shit. Lil Tony made his way in their direction.

"What's good with the guys?" Lil Tony greeted, shaking hands with the homies.

"Aye, big fella, let me holla at you real quick, G," Lil Tony said to Big Nasty in a jolly voice.

Big Nasty looked at Lil Tony through his bloodshot eyes. He was high as a kite on K-2. "What's up? Speak on it," Big Nasty said dryly.

"This ain't for everybody, big homie. I'm trying to put you on something to put some stamps in your pocket." At the mention of *stamps in your pocket*, Big Nasty got off the bench.

Thirsty ass nigga, Lil Tony thought.

"Come on, G. Let's spend a lap real quick," Lil Tony said.

Lil Tony and Big Nasty dipped off to walk a few laps.

"Check it out, G. I know you already hip to me and Kilo having them squares," Lil Tony stated as he and Big Nasty walked side by side.

"Yeah, I'm hip. I'm also hip to how you niggas ain't been feeding the guys. But if niggas get into some funk the guys gon' be the first one y'all run to in order to save y'all," Big Nasty replied full of hate and envy.

"First and foremost, Lil Tony don't run from no rec or work call! Secondly, we ain't got enough to feed the guys. As you know, everybody ain't got that hustle bone in their body. We don't have it just to be giving to nigga's that's gon' fuck up the money. Everything ain't for everybody, that's why I'm hollering at you now. I already know you a hustla and you about that money. So, me and my celly figured we would front you a pouch. You bring us thirty books and you keep thirty books. That's fair ain't it?" Lil Tony said, stroking Big Nasty's ego.

He knew Big Nasty was nothing related to a hustla, he was a K-2 head. Lil Tony had even heard that Big Nasty was on the unit selling shit out of his locker to get high, including his hygiene items. Big Nasty was nothing but a dope fiend, strung out on K-2. But the fact of the matter was, Lil Tony had to rock him to sleep if he wanted everything to go smoothly.

"Hell yeah, that's fair, G. When you gon' give it to me?" Big Nasty inquired.

The stamps he was going to make from the squares were already spent in his mind on K-2.

"When they call the move, slide to my unit. I've got to bag the shit up for you. Or you can just wait until the morning and I can bring it to breakfast?" Lil Tony asked him, already knowing the answer.

"Nah, we ain't got to wait 'til the morning, G. We can slide when they call the move, my nigga," Big Nasty replied like he and Lil Tony were best friends from the sandbox.

It's funny how a jealous-hearted individual who despises you and everything you do, can turn into your ride or die homie once you say you gon' give them something that's going to benefit them, Lil Tony thought.

Thirty minutes later, the 1:30 move was called. Lil Tony and Big Nasty left the yard headed to D-block, Lil Tony's unit. Walking in the unit, Lil Tony led Big Nasty to his cell. Coming in the cell Lil Tony was greeted by the strong smell of alcohol. Kilo and Jazzy were in the cell sipping on shine and smoking cigarettes. This was all a part of the bloody plot. Zimmer, the white boy rapper from South Dakota, had let Lil Tony know he had come down with another batch of some jail house shine he was trying to sell for five books. Light bulbs went off in Lil Tony's head. If he got Big Nasty drunk and high, he would be all the way off his square, which would make it that much easier to bring him the move that was about to be brought to him. Lil Tony gave Zimmer six squares for the potent liquid. Kilo and Jazzy were just setting the stage for what was about to happen.

"What's good, big G?" Kilo greeted, seeing Big Nasty enter the cell with Lil Tony.

"What up, Lord? I ain't know you and Lil Tony was cellies," Big Nasty said truthfully.

"Yeah, that's my man's. You wanna hit this?" Kilo asked offering Big Nasty the water bottle with the clear liquid in it.

"Hell yeah!" Big Nasty said accepting the bottle from Kilo and taking a strong swig before trying to hand it back.

"Nah, G go ahead and hit that muthafucka," Kilo encouraged.

Big Nasty took another strong sip as Lil Tony was in his locker bagging up a couple of caps of tobacco. After doing so, he gave Big Nasty six caps—a pouch.

"Here, G, that's for you. Remember bring back thirty books and we gon' flood you with some more," Lil Tony assured him.

"I got you, fam," Big Nasty replied weakly.

He was already starting to feel the effects of the liquor immediately. While Big Nasty continued to get his drink on, Lil Tony sat at the small desk in the cell rolling up cigarettes. In one of them was a little bit of tobacco, the rest was chopped up pieces of K-2. He passed Kilo a rolled square, then Jazzy. He gave the one with the K-2 in it to Big Nasty. He was bubbly. Kilo used two batteries and a piece of wire to light a twisted piece of toilet paper. In the jail, this was equivalent to a Bic lighter.

After getting the tissue lit, he used it to light the tip of his cigarette, then he passed the torch to Jazzy. After Jazzy lit his square, he held the flame out to Big Nasty to allow him to light his square. Once Big Nasty had his shit lit, Jazzy tossed the flame in the toilet. The half of bottle of shine had Big Nasty slightly tipsy, so he took a drag from the cigarette. Before he knew it, he was higher than a giraffe's pussy.

Jazzy took a swig from his bottle. In his pocket was a padlock with a braided shoestring tied to it. All he was waiting on was for the move to be called so he could put it to work. Big Nasty finished the K-2 cigarette in three strong pulls. The drug began to run its course on the big fella. He began to sweat profusely, and it felt as if his insides were about to erupt.

His world began to spin as he grabbed his stomach and made a quick movement to the toilet inside the cell. Vomit shot out of his mouth like a volcano into the toilet as he emptied everything he'd eaten that day. Lil Tony glanced over at him as he had an episode. He rolled another cigarette laced with the dangerous drug. Jazzy stood by the door to watch out for the C.O. He was starting to sweat from anticipation of putting in the work on Big Nasty. He wasn't scared or nervous, it was anticipation.

Five minutes after all the throwing up and dry heaving, Big Nasty sat in the chair high as a kite. While he was on his knees praying to the porcelain god, Lil Tony told Jazzy to go in Big Nasty's pocket to relieve him of the tobacco he had just given him, in which he did.

"Here, drink some water, G," Kilo said, handing Big Nasty the water bottle with the shine in it.

Big Nasty squirted the bottle in his mouth, he was trashed. Lil Tony used this time to spark the freshly rolled K-2 cigarette. He faked like he was taking a pull but didn't inhale before he passed it to Big Nasty.

"Here, fam, smoke this. The cigarette is going to bring the high down," Lil Tony lied.

Big Nasty didn't know what was going on around him. He accepted the square and took a pull. He was trembling and sweating as his heart beat out his chest. He hit the K-2 once more before he went back at it with the toilet. When he finished, he sat back in the chair staring into space.

"What time is it, Jazzy?" Lil Tony asked.

Jazzy looked at his G-shock watch. "It's two-twenty—they about to call the move in ten minutes," Jazzy replied.

"Good. He should have come down by then. At least enough to walk," Lil Tony retorted!

Ten minutes later, the 2:30, five-minute move was called.

"Come on, G. That's the move," Lil Tony said helping Big Nasty to his feet.

"You good, bro?" Jazzy asked him.

"Yeah—I'm good," Big Nasty replied high as hell.

His mobile skills were way slower than normal as he made his way toward the front door of the unit. The Correctional Officer was outside serving the front of the building while the move was on. Jazzy was walking behind Big Nasty. He used this time to make his move as he discreetly pulled the lock out of his pocket and wrapped it tightly around his fist.

"Aye, Big Nasty!" Jazzy said calling his name.

Big Nasty looked back at the same time Jazzy swung the lock as hard as he could. The lock swinging through the air sounded like a whistle before it connected with Big Nasty's forehead. *Crack!* The sound was deafening. Big Nasty stumbled back from the powerful blow. He saw a bright light. The skin on his forehead separated, exposing white flesh before blood squirted out of it. Big Nasty's vision went black as he tumbled to the floor like a tree, he was knocked out cold.

Jazzy continued to rain blow upon blow to Big Nasty's exposed face, breaking his nose, eye socket, jaw, and anything else pertaining to his face. To say Jazzy had given him a face lift would be an understatement. When the C.O. walked back into the unit, Jazzy was still beating Big Nasty to a bloody pulp. The C.O. hit his body alarm, pulled his pepper spray from his utility belt, ran over, and started spraying Jazzy. Jazzy ceased his vicious assault and got away from the pepper spray that was blinding him and had him coughing up his lungs. A few seconds later, the unit was swarmed with C.O.s in riot gear.

"Lock in a fucking cell—lock-in—lock-in!" They yelled with authority.

Jazzy was handcuffed by two C.O.s and taken out of the unit on his way to the SHU. Big Nasty laid on the ground with his brains oozing out different parts of his melon. He had to be loaded on a stretcher and then flown out of the prison by Med-Flight, which was a waste of fuel, the nigga was already dead. This nigga Jazzy had just caught a body, but what the fuck did he care. He was twenty-six years old and already serving life.

Chapter 30

Lil Tony: A Week Later

On my mama this nigga Jazzy went crazy! I knew shorty went hard in the paint but damn, I didn't think he was gon' beat Big Nasty to death. We had been on lockdown for a week after the incident. We were supposed to come off lockdown status after 4:00 count. I wasn't tripping on being locked in a cell. It was a righteous call that needed to happen in order for the organization to flourish into something great. I kept replaying the violence over and over in my head and it gave me a sense of satisfaction.

Big Nasty deserved what happened to him. I was subordinate to our big homie and his teachings, but the way Big Nasty moved went against everything we stood for. While on this lockdown, me and Kilo managed to sell out all the tobacco we had and were loaded with stamps. Since niggas in our unit knew we had the squares, we stayed fishing under the door. Fishing was the only way to get shit from each other on the lockdown. We used a tube of empty toothpaste, poked a small hole at the end of it, and tied a string through the hole that we got from our blanket, this was called a line. Once the line was made, we would slide the toothpaste tube under the door, down the tier.

The person we were trying to connect with, would sling his toothpaste tube under his door with a staple on the front of it. The staple would catch on the line and he would pull my toothpaste tube in his cell. Whatever we were trying to send would be tied to the line and that's how we passed shit. This technique would get mastered only through doing time and I had it mastered it. C.O. Jenkins had also been working our unit during the lockdown. My celly had this bitch's mind gone and he hadn't even fucked her.

A few days ago, while we were in the shower, C.O. Jenkins searched our cell. When we got back in the cell Kilo happened to look under his pillow only to see that this freak bitch had left her panties. The first thing he did was smell them. He smiled before he passed them to me and them bitches smelled like fish and vinegar—

straight up! But one thing about C.O. Jenkins's funky ass, she was willing to make some money, which was the only thing that mattered. Once we got out of this cell I was going right to the phone to call K.T., then I was going to the yard. I had some unfinished Nation business to stand on with Lil Folks.

After the 4:00 count was cleared, the C.O.s came around to let us out of our cells. A lot of inmates rushed to the showers, some to the computers to check their emails and some of us went to the phones. I went to the phone. I was lucky to be one of the first ones, that way I wouldn't have to stand in a long ass line. I grabbed the phone and dialed my cousin K.T.'s number. He answered on the third ring and the automated voice recorder came on letting us know that the call was being monitored and all that bullshit.

"What's the business, G?" K.T. greeted over the line.

"Man, what's good? Where the fuck you at?" I probed, hearing the loud bass from the music in the background.

"I'm at a strip club in Madison, Wisconsin. What's up, you good?" K.T. said, loud as hell so I could hear him over the music.

"Hell naw, Aye?"

"What's up?"

"Remember baby mama called you for that lil' bread?"

"Yeah."

"Aye, she gon' call you again. My son needs some gym shoes. Get him a pair of Jordan's, the Retro 4s," I said in code. He knew the 4 meant D for dope.

"How many pairs shorty need?"

"Just get him one for right now," I said. K.T. knew I meant an ounce.

"Alright, say no more, fam," he replied.

Me and K.T. talked for a few more minutes before we ended the call. I didn't want to keep him tied up while he was out kicking it. Plus, while I was on the phone, I heard the C.O. announce it was about to be a 5:00 move called, and I had some shit to do before I went outside. I went into my cell, went in my pillow, and got my knife. After I got my weapon, I was getting a stack of magazines from off the floor when Kilo came into the cell from just using the computer.

"We outside when they call the move, G?" he asked me.

"Hell yeah, aye I need you to call Swift G in here real quick," I told him.

Kilo did as I requested as I slid my white T-shirt from over my torso, then went in my locker to get a roll of electrical tape that I got from a white boy who worked on the safety crew.

"What's up, G?" Swift said as he entered my cell. Kilo was behind him.

"We about to go out here and handle this Nation business. You ready?" I asked Swift, trying to see if he was still on the same page he was before the lockdown. Swift G pulled two shanks off his waist as if they were Glocks.

"I'm with the righteous," Swift replied.

I smiled, loving his loyalty to the MOB.

"GD then, my nigga! Aye, help me wrap these around my stomach," I said, giving the stack of magazines to Swift.

For the next ten minutes, Swift and Kilo taped magazines around my stomach and lower chest. This was equivalent to having on a bulletproof vest. I was aware it was a possibility some of the men would side with Lil Folks, and at the sight of Lil Folks' blood being spilled it could possibly ignite a war, so I was getting war-ready. The homies had just finished what they were doing just as the 5:00 move was called. I slid my white T-shirt back on and put on a brown khaki shirt over it.

"Kilo, make sure you have the Lords in position just in case we need some aid and assist," I said while buttoning up my khaki shirt.

"I got you, fam! What needs to be said don't need to be explained," Kilo retorted.

"Then say no more, let's ride," I said, tucking my knife and walking out of my cell.

When I got on the yard, I looked in the direction toward the bench where the guys were. It was a lot of men out today. I happened to see Lil Folks waving his hands around like he was dictating. I saw Scrill over there as well and made my way to the bench,

Kilo and Swift at my side. As I approached, Lil Folks turned his attention to me, a mean mug on his face.

"What the fuck happened to Big Nasty? He's dead and y'all coming on the yard, make that make sense," Lil Folks said through clenched teeth.

A lot of the men had hard aggressive looks on their faces. I had to make my move now before shit went left. I had to take initiative. I looked over at Scrill catching eye contact, letting him know, *let's get to it.*

"Hold up, G, we gon' get to that. First, let's get to this." Scrill took some papers out of his pockets and unfolded them.

"Thousands of pardons, fam. I would like to read something to the membership," Scrill said, holding up the paper. Without waiting for acknowledgment he began to read. "*Beginning in May two-thousand-eight, or earlier, Defendant Antonio Ramon Parker, reached an agreement with the United States District Attorney to cooperate with the information pertaining to the hearing indictment. It was said to be true that the defendant with others including, but not limited to Lamont Christens, Charles P.A. Fountain, and Maurice Henderson, conspired to rob Brinks Financial, in which an employee was killed. This violation of 18.U.S.C 924-C apply. The mandatory minimum penalty is life in prison and the maximum penalty of death by lethal injection.*

Specifically, on May tenth of two-thousand-eight, you and others attempted to rob Brinks Financial. You and others fired several rounds at Brinks employees, killing one, Deangelo Pierce. The defendant hereby certifies that the facts set forth above are true and accurate to the best of his knowledge. Signed Antonio Ramon Parker," Scrill finished reading Lil Folks' statement of facts pertaining to his case.

"On the, G, you hot ass!" One of the guys named, Spody G, said in disbelief.

Spody had been indicted out of Iowa and was giving a life sentence for heroin.

Lil Folks didn't know what to say, "Tha-tha-that ain't my paperwork," he stuttered like a muthafucka.

"Hold up, family, I ain't done," Scrill said, unfolding another piece of paper. I already knew what the business was, so I moved closer to where Lil Folks was standing, discreetly.

"This right here is an email from the big homie Big Cliff. After I read this it will be passed around to all the guys. If you want to verify the email you will have forty-eight hours to do so. The email address is on the paper. You can holla at Big Cliff yourself." Scrill began to read the email, *"To my beloved family, I come as a representative of our chairman and all of his teachings. You all know there is a leadership code of conduct, we have made the claim of being Special People, us leaders must convey this to the membership by our words and conduct. We must live the concept. I will treat the men, in the same manner, I would want to be treated. But as a leader, I will do it first, in actions, thoughts, and words, we must all keep in mind that the membership makes us leader, and as we guide them—so shall they follow. We must not all live by these teachings. The individual who claims I have given him the authority to hold the title of overseer is fictitious in his doings. Disension and insubordinate acts are frowned upon. This individual has relished in this manner—"* Scrill stopped reading only to look in the faces of the men. I slickly pulled my knife out, holding it in my coat sleeve, moving even closer to Lil Folks. Scrill continued to read, *"This individual is to be dealt with as an enemy of the people."*

I was standing next to Lil Folks when I grabbed him, pulled him forcefully toward me, and stuck his ass in three quick rapid sessions. I looked him in his eyes as I did this. I could feel the steel popping through his coat, as well as his flesh. Lil Folks had a look of horror as I pushed him away from me. I then looked at Hell-Boy while I held the shank that was dripping with Lil Folks' blood.

"Hell-Boy, walk this nigga to the gate, I commanded, now testing Hell-Boy's loyalty. If he didn't do it, I was gon' blast his ass, too. Like I figured he would do, Hell-Boy briskly walked over to Lil Folks as he clutched his stomach trying to stop the bleeding, and punched Lil Folks in the jaw, breaking it.

"Get your police ass off the yard," Hell-Boy said through clenched teeth.

Another one of the guys who went by the name of R.T. pulled a knife out as he advanced towards Lil Folks.

"Hit that gate bitch ass nigga before we kill your ass," R.T. threatened.

R.T was from Racine, Wisconsin, and was already serving eighty years for a body he caught in the feds. Lil Folks stumbled back trying to get away from the venomous situation he was in. His midsection was on fire from the three puncture wounds he had just received.

"Alright, fam, y'all—got that," Lil Folks said weakly and staggered to the fence as sharp pains shot through his body.

Hell-Boy trailed behind him for security purposes, just in case he tried to buck. The C.O. standing on the other side of the fence saw the bloody wounded inmate walking in his direction and hit his body alarm. Moments later, medical staff and correctional officers descended from the administration building, rushing to the yard. Lil Folks police ass told the C.O.s he could no longer be on the compound. They escorted his ass to the SHU, but first, he had to go to medical so they could attend to that work call I just gave him. I just handled that Nation business.

The officer in the gun tower called yard recall over the intercom while sticking an AR-15 out the window to make sure all the inmates complied and exited the yard. I cautiously handed Swift G the bloody knife. We walked separate directions just in case the camera caught the stabbing. I had to get the weapon off me. I nodded my head to the guys.

"Love folks!" I heard a few of them say as we went our separate ways to our units.

Them saying that to me was them showing me respect. They respected the move I had just put down. When we came back in the unit, the C.O.s demanded that we lock in our cells, in which we obliged. We had just come off lockdown and were going right back. The leader of the GDs had just got punished and ran up. The administration was definitely about to investigate and try to find out the motive for what just happened. About forty-five minutes after we had been locked in our cells, C.O.s swarmed the unit, marching toward my cell. I was already anticipating them coming.

"Here they come, Kilo," I told my celly, putting him on point.

The C.O.s stopped in front of my cell and opened the food slot.

"Anthony Banks, cuff up!" the C.O. said with authority.

Me and Kilo gave each other some dap.

"Hurry up and get me out, Lord," I told Kilo.

"Don't even trip, G, I got you," Kilo replied.

I bent down and stuck my hands out of the food slot. Cold handcuffs were slapped around my wrist. The CO opened my cell door and pulled me out. I was taken to the Special Housing Unit. After being processed in the SHU, I was led to my cell right next door to Black Mac and his celly Stackhouse. Black Mac was looking out the cell window smiling at me while I waited for the C.O.s to unlock my cell. Black Mac was happy to see me.

"What up, ock?" he said through the door.

"I'm good. How are you, fam?" I asked as I stood handcuffed behind my back.

"All is well," he replied.

The C.O. let me in my cell. I was lucky to be getting my own cell. I wasn't really in the mood to have a celly. Once inside my cell, my handcuffs were taken off and my cell locked.

After the C.O.s left, Black Mac wasted no time, "Lil Tony, what happened?" He eagerly inquired out the door.

I went to the door and answered, "I'm 'bout to send you a kite."

I knew niggas were on the tier listening, so I figured that I would just write it down. It was Nation business, so I had to keep it like that. I had folks send me something to write with. After giving them the brief synopsis of the situation, I slid the kite under the door and fished it in.

"Lil Tony, what's good, G?" Stackhouse yelled out to me.

"Stackhouse, what's up folks! I'm all good, just had to stand on that business. I wrote it on the kite."

After they read the kite, they had an understanding on what went down. They knew I was back there on Nation business. The administration gave me a disciplinary shot for assault. I wasn't tripping. Sometimes, sacrifices had to be made. Black Mac told me to sign up for recreation in the morning, so I could go out to the cage with them, and we could holla face to face without niggas being all in our business.

"That's a bet," I replied.

I made up my bed, then plopped down on my bunk. Today had been action-packed. I was in the SHU for putting in some work. Not only did the camera capture the stabbing, but Lil Folks hot ass told on me. I clasped my hands behind my head and closed my eyes. A feeling of power floated through my veins, had my morale up. But me getting stuck in prison for politicks put a sense of worry on my mind frame. I had only been locked up for thirteen months with a lot more time to serve. I had to get my shit established so I could just focus on getting back to the crib.

Chapter 31

K.T.

The sound of *Lil Baby's* new track *Woah* pounded through the speakers, set up around Visions strip club in Madison, Wisconsin. I was getting an X-rated lap dance from a petite female by the name of Lil Red. I had been fucking with shorty for a minute. Lil Red was a white chick about 5'1, with red hair and a body like one of those bitches in the Curve magazine, on gang! Lil Red was grinding on my dick getting the front of my Dior jeans soaking wet from her pussy juice. I wasn't tripping, even though I paid 2500 for the jeans, that wasn't shit.

Lil Red was attempting to unbuckle my Hermes belt buckle when my iPhone vibrated in the pocket of my Tom Ford jacket. I looked at the screen and saw it was my cousin Lil Tony calling, so I answered as I tried to pry Lil Red off my dick. Me and Lil Tony talked for a few minutes with him giving me the business and what needed to be done. We ended our call. My cousin was in the feds trying to shake a bag. I was just happy to be a part of it. While Lil Red continued to grind on my meat, I saw Kevin sitting at the bar with some thick chocolate bitch on his lap. I could see his jewelry shining from all the way across the club.

I was proud of Kevin. I plugged him with some of my people who were doing big things with the loud. I invested a hunnid gees and Kevin took off. He conducted himself righteously, made some big boy moves, and got his weight up. His finger was still a little itchy, so if need be, and a nigga got out his lane, I would send Kevin to come blow something down. Other than that, we were getting to the money.

In Bloomington, I was seeing about thirty racks a day, and that was gram for gram. Bloomington was just my headquarters, as I had workers in other cities getting money for me. Madison, Rockford, Illinois, Chicago, Detroit, Minnesota to South Dakota. My hustla mind-frame had me a giant out here. I was fucking them up. I was thinking about taking Lil Red to the Crown Plaza hotel and digging her guts out but quickly changed my mind. Fuck that, I was going home to my girl tonight. I had finally realized Tiff was the only one I wanted.

Her loyalty, support, and navigation through the bullshit she had to go through, to love a nigga like me, let me know that she was the one. I was already looking at something icy to put around her finger. I looked at a Robert Coin Savage Priv. It was white gold and flooded with diamonds. It was a 1-carat engagement ring. The check on it was 110 bands. As a matter of fact, first thing in the morning, I was going to the diamond district to snatch that for baby, on me! I was about to wife Tiff.

After getting my lap dance, I reached in my pocket and pulled out a knot of money. It was about 7300 in small bills. I peeled off a stack and handed it to Lil Red. She looked at me like she was disappointed. She wanted some dick, but tonight I wasn't on that. Nevertheless, her thirsty ass took the stack. I got up and made my way over to Kevin, who had just popped a bottle of 1738. My x pill was kicking in and I needed some liquor to even it out.

As I made my way to the bar, I caught eyes with a familiar face. It didn't take long to recall where I had seen the face. I remembered the face vividly. He was the nigga with the dreads in the car when I served Boo. The nigga had a smirk on his face. He looked in my direction then made his way over to the stage to throw some money. Something in my gut was telling me something was up with dude.

"Aye, fam, let's get up outta here," I said, walking up to Kevin.

"What's up, you good?" he asked, getting the stripper off his lap and standing up getting on point.

"Nah, I wanna see something real quick. Let's bounce."

Kevin grabbed the bottle of Remy and we left out the club. My 'Lac truck was parked across the street in the parking lot of Prime Quarters Steakhouse.

"Man, what's up, fam?" Kevin probed, once we were behind tint.

"This nigga in the club gave me a bad vibe. I wanna see something," I told Kevin.

Not even a second later the nigga came out the front door of Visions, he was looking around like he was looking for somebody before he walked over to a dark-colored Tahoe and got in. I hit the push button, bringing the Escalade engine to life. I waited till he pulled out of Visions parking lot and made a right on East Washington Street. I calmly pulled out of the lot of Prime Quarters and began to tail his ass.

"You got that pipe on you?" I asked Kevin.

"Yeah, we good," he replied, reaching under the seat, then putting a 21-shot FNH handgun on his lap.

I tailed the Tahoe all the way to the Westside of Madison to a neighborhood and street called Allied Drive.

"Let me see that," I told Kevin.

Kevin handed me the FN as the Tahoe pulled into an apartment complex and parked. I slowly drove past. I parked three cars down. I didn't know who this nigga was or what he was on, but I was definitely about to find out. I pulled the slide back on the FN, chambering a 5.62 round into the chamber before I stepped out the whip.

Chapter 32

Kilo

"Check!" I said, using my bishop to threaten his king.

I was playing chess with one of the Bloods named Bando from Atlanta. I could hardly concentrate. I was sick about my celly being in the SHU. We had a lot going on with this C.O. bitch and getting to this paper, but we knew this could possibly be the outcome from all the politicking. Damn, it was always something. The same day Lil Tony went to the hole, H.D. was released from the hole. His ass was on thin ice. I sat and had a man-to-man talk with him and told him how I felt about him smoking that K-2 shit. That shit'll bring the worst out of you and I wanted him to see that. Vice Lords are better than that. I let K.D. know that another episode like that and he was gone on the fin!

Bando used a pawn to block his king out of check, my rook now exposed by his queen. I was concentrating on my next move when C.O.s came into the unit escorting four new inmates. All the men in the dayroom turned their attention to the new arrivals. Immediately, I spotted a nigga I knew from the streets this hoe ass nigga named Bud was coming on the unit. The hoe ass nigga that set me up with the feds. This had to be a setup, I thought.

"What's wrong, Lord?" Bando asked.

I stood from the table and rushed to my cell to get my knife. Ain't no way this hot ass vic was gon' stay on this compound—not without bleeding.

To Be Continued...
Bred in the Game 2
Coming Soon

Submission Guideline

Submit the first three chapters of your completed manuscript to ldpsubmissions@gmail.com, subject line: Your book's title. The manuscript must be in a .doc file and sent as an attachment. Document should be in Times New Roman, double spaced and in size 12 font. Also, provide your synopsis and full contact information. If sending multiple submissions, they must each be in a separate email.

Have a story but no way to send it electronically? You can still submit to LDP/Ca$h Presents. Send in the first three chapters, written or typed, of your completed manuscript to:

LDP: Submissions Dept
Po Box 944
Stockbridge, Ga 30281

DO NOT send original manuscript. Must be a duplicate.

Provide your synopsis and a cover letter containing your full contact information.

Thanks for considering LDP and Ca$h Presents.

Coming Soon from Lock Down Publications/Ca$h Presents

BOW DOWN TO MY GANGSTA

By **Ca$h**

TORN BETWEEN TWO

By **Coffee**

BLOOD OF A BOSS **VI**

SHADOWS OF THE GAME II

TRAP BASTARD II

By **Askari**

LOYAL TO THE GAME **IV**

By **T.J. & Jelissa**

IF LOVING YOU IS WRONG… **III**

By **Jelissa**

TRUE SAVAGE **VIII**

MIDNIGHT CARTEL IV

DOPE BOY MAGIC IV

CITY OF KINGZ III

By **Chris Green**

BLAST FOR ME **III**

A SAVAGE DOPEBOY III

CUTTHROAT MAFIA III

DUFFLE BAG CARTEL VI

HEARTLESS GOON VI

By **Ghost**

A HUSTLER'S DECEIT III

KILL ZONE **II**

BAE BELONGS TO ME III

A DOPE BOY'S QUEEN III

By **Aryanna**

COKE KINGS V

KING OF THE TRAP III

By **T.J. Edwards**

GORILLAZ IN THE BAY V

3X KRAZY III

De'Kari

THE STREETS ARE CALLING II

Duquie Wilson

KINGPIN KILLAZ IV

STREET KINGS III

PAID IN BLOOD III

CARTEL KILLAZ IV

DOPE GODS III

Hood Rich

SINS OF A HUSTLA II

ASAD

KINGZ OF THE GAME VI

Playa Ray

SLAUGHTER GANG IV

RUTHLESS HEART IV

By Willie Slaughter

FUK SHYT II

By Blakk Diamond

TRAP QUEEN

RICH $AVAGE II

By Troublesome

YAYO V

GHOST MOB II

Stilloan Robinson

CREAM III

By Yolanda Moore

SON OF A DOPE FIEND III

HEAVEN GOT A GHETTO II

By Renta

FOREVER GANGSTA II

GLOCKS ON SATIN SHEETS III

By Adrian Dulan

LOYALTY AIN'T PROMISED III

By Keith Williams

THE PRICE YOU PAY FOR LOVE III

By Destiny Skai

I'M NOTHING WITHOUT HIS LOVE II

SINS OF A THUG II

TO THE THUG I LOVED BEFORE II

By Monet Dragun

LIFE OF A SAVAGE IV

MURDA SEASON IV

GANGLAND CARTEL IV

CHI'RAQ GANGSTAS IV

KILLERS ON ELM STREET IV

JACK BOYZ N DA BRONX III

A DOPEBOY'S DREAM II

By **Romell Tukes**

QUIET MONEY IV

EXTENDED CLIP III

THUG LIFE IV

By **Trai'Quan**

THE STREETS MADE ME III

By **Larry D. Wright**

IF YOU CROSS ME ONCE II

ANGEL III

By **Anthony Fields**

FRIEND OR FOE III

By **Mimi**

SAVAGE STORMS III

By **Meesha**

BLOOD ON THE MONEY III

By J-Blunt

THE STREETS WILL NEVER CLOSE II

By K'ajji

NIGHTMARES OF A HUSTLA III

By King Dream

IN THE ARM OF HIS BOSS

By Jamila

HARD AND RUTHLESS III

MOB TOWN 251 II

By Von Diesel

LEVELS TO THIS SHYT II

By Ah'Million

MOB TIES III

By SayNoMore

THE LAST OF THE OGS III

Tranay Adams

FOR THE LOVE OF A BOSS II

By C. D. Blue

MOBBED UP II

By King Rio

BRED IN THE GAME II

By S. Allen

Available Now

RESTRAINING ORDER **I & II**

By **CA$H & Coffee**

LOVE KNOWS NO BOUNDARIES **I II & III**

By **Coffee**

RAISED AS A GOON I, II, III & IV

BRED BY THE SLUMS I, II, III

BLAST FOR ME I & II

ROTTEN TO THE CORE I II III

A BRONX TALE I, II, III

DUFFLE BAG CARTEL I II III IV V

HEARTLESS GOON I II III IV V

A SAVAGE DOPEBOY I II

DRUG LORDS I II III

CUTTHROAT MAFIA I II

By **Ghost**

LAY IT DOWN **I & II**

LAST OF A DYING BREED I II

BLOOD STAINS OF A SHOTTA I & II III

By **Jamaica**

LOYAL TO THE GAME I II III

LIFE OF SIN I, II III

By **TJ & Jelissa**

BLOODY COMMAS I & II

SKI MASK CARTEL I II & III

KING OF NEW YORK I II,III IV V

RISE TO POWER I II III

COKE KINGS I II III IV

BORN HEARTLESS I II III IV

KING OF THE TRAP I II

By **T.J. Edwards**

IF LOVING HIM IS WRONG…I & II

LOVE ME EVEN WHEN IT HURTS I II III

By **Jelissa**

WHEN THE STREETS CLAP BACK I & II III

THE HEART OF A SAVAGE I II III

By **Jibril Williams**

A DISTINGUISHED THUG STOLE MY HEART I II & III

LOVE SHOULDN'T HURT I II III IV

RENEGADE BOYS I II III IV

PAID IN KARMA I II III

SAVAGE STORMS I II

By **Meesha**

A GANGSTER'S CODE I &, II III

A GANGSTER'S SYN I II III

THE SAVAGE LIFE I II III

CHAINED TO THE STREETS I II III

BLOOD ON THE MONEY I II

By J-Blunt

PUSH IT TO THE LIMIT

By **Bre' Hayes**

BLOOD OF A BOSS **I, II, III, IV, V**

SHADOWS OF THE GAME

TRAP BASTARD

By **Askari**

THE STREETS BLEED MURDER **I, II & III**

THE HEART OF A GANGSTA I II& III

By **Jerry Jackson**

CUM FOR ME I II III IV V VI VII

An **LDP Erotica Collaboration**

BRIDE OF A HUSTLA **I II & II**

THE FETTI GIRLS **I, II& III**

CORRUPTED BY A GANGSTA I, II III, IV

BLINDED BY HIS LOVE

THE PRICE YOU PAY FOR LOVE I II

DOPE GIRL MAGIC I II III

By **Destiny Skai**

WHEN A GOOD GIRL GOES BAD

By **Adrienne**

THE COST OF LOYALTY I II III

By Kweli

A GANGSTER'S REVENGE **I II III & IV**

THE BOSS MAN'S DAUGHTERS I II III IV V

A SAVAGE LOVE **I & II**

BAE BELONGS TO ME I II

A HUSTLER'S DECEIT I, II, III

WHAT BAD BITCHES DO I, II, III

SOUL OF A MONSTER I II III

KILL ZONE

A DOPE BOY'S QUEEN I II

By **Aryanna**

A KINGPIN'S AMBITON

A KINGPIN'S AMBITION **II**

I MURDER FOR THE DOUGH

By **Ambitious**

TRUE SAVAGE I II III IV V VI VII

DOPE BOY MAGIC I, II, III

MIDNIGHT CARTEL I II III

CITY OF KINGZ I II

By **Chris Green**

A DOPEBOY'S PRAYER

By **Eddie "Wolf" Lee**

THE KING CARTEL **I, II & III**

By **Frank Gresham**

THESE NIGGAS AIN'T LOYAL **I, II & III**

By **Nikki Tee**

GANGSTA SHYT **I II &III**

By **CATO**

THE ULTIMATE BETRAYAL

By **Phoenix**

BOSS'N UP **I , II & III**

By **Royal Nicole**

I LOVE YOU TO DEATH

By Destiny J

I RIDE FOR MY HITTA

I STILL RIDE FOR MY HITTA

By **Misty Holt**

LOVE & CHASIN' PAPER

By **Qay Crockett**

TO DIE IN VAIN

SINS OF A HUSTLA

By **ASAD**

BROOKLYN HUSTLAZ

By **Boogsy Morina**

BROOKLYN ON LOCK I & II

By **Sonovia**

GANGSTA CITY

By **Teddy Duke**

A DRUG KING AND HIS DIAMOND I & II III

A DOPEMAN'S RICHES

HER MAN, MINE'S TOO I, II

CASH MONEY HO'S

THE WIFEY I USED TO BE I II

By Nicole Goosby

TRAPHOUSE KING **I II & III**

KINGPIN KILLAZ I II III

STREET KINGS I II

PAID IN BLOOD **I II**

CARTEL KILLAZ I II III

DOPE GODS I II

By **Hood Rich**

LIPSTICK KILLAH **I, II, III**

CRIME OF PASSION I II & III

FRIEND OR FOE I II

By **Mimi**

STEADY MOBBN' **I, II, III**

THE STREETS STAINED MY SOUL I II

By **Marcellus Allen**

WHO SHOT YA **I, II, III**

SON OF A DOPE FIEND I II

HEAVEN GOT A GHETTO

Renta

GORILLAZ IN THE BAY **I II III IV**

TEARS OF A GANGSTA I II

3X KRAZY I II

DE'KARI

TRIGGADALE I II III

Elijah R. Freeman

GOD BLESS THE TRAPPERS I, II, III

THESE SCANDALOUS STREETS I, II, III

FEAR MY GANGSTA I, II, III IV, V

THESE STREETS DON'T LOVE NOBODY I, II

BURY ME A G I, II, III, IV, V

A GANGSTA'S EMPIRE I, II, III, IV

THE DOPEMAN'S BODYGAURD I II

THE REALEST KILLAZ I II III

THE LAST OF THE OGS I II

Tranay Adams

THE STREETS ARE CALLING

Duquie Wilson

MARRIED TO A BOSS… I II III

By Destiny Skai & Chris Green

KINGZ OF THE GAME I II III IV V

Playa Ray

SLAUGHTER GANG I II III

RUTHLESS HEART I II III

By Willie Slaughter

FUK SHYT

By Blakk Diamond

DON'T F#CK WITH MY HEART I II

By Linnea

ADDICTED TO THE DRAMA I II III

IN THE ARM OF HIS BOSS II

By Jamila

YAYO I II III IV

A SHOOTER'S AMBITION I II

BRED IN THE GAME

By S. Allen

TRAP GOD I II III

RICH $AVAGE

By Troublesome

FOREVER GANGSTA

GLOCKS ON SATIN SHEETS I II

By Adrian Dulan

TOE TAGZ I II III

LEVELS TO THIS SHYT

By Ah'Million

KINGPIN DREAMS I II III

By Paper Boi Rari

CONFESSIONS OF A GANGSTA I II III

By Nicholas Lock

I'M NOTHING WITHOUT HIS LOVE

SINS OF A THUG

TO THE THUG I LOVED BEFORE

By Monet Dragun

CAUGHT UP IN THE LIFE I II III

By Robert Baptiste

NEW TO THE GAME I II III

MONEY, MURDER & MEMORIES I II III

By **Malik D. Rice**

LIFE OF A SAVAGE I II III

A GANGSTA'S QUR'AN I II III

MURDA SEASON I II III

GANGLAND CARTEL I II III

CHI'RAQ GANGSTAS I II III

KILLERS ON ELM STREET I II III

JACK BOYZ N DA BRONX I II

A DOPEBOY'S DREAM

By **Romell Tukes**

LOYALTY AIN'T PROMISED I II

By Keith Williams

QUIET MONEY I II III

THUG LIFE I II III

EXTENDED CLIP I II

By **Trai'Quan**

THE STREETS MADE ME I II

By **Larry D. Wright**

THE ULTIMATE SACRIFICE I, II, III, IV, V, VI

KHADIFI

IF YOU CROSS ME ONCE

ANGEL I II

IN THE BLINK OF AN EYE

By **Anthony Fields**

THE LIFE OF A HOOD STAR

By Ca$h & Rashia Wilson

THE STREETS WILL NEVER CLOSE

By K'ajji

CREAM I II

By Yolanda Moore

NIGHTMARES OF A HUSTLA I II

By King Dream

CONCRETE KILLA I II

By Kingpen

HARD AND RUTHLESS I II

MOB TOWN 251

By Von Diesel

GHOST MOB II

Stilloan Robinson

MOB TIES I II

By SayNoMore

BODYMORE MURDERLAND I II III

By Delmont Player

FOR THE LOVE OF A BOSS

By C. D. Blue

MOBBED UP

By King Rio

BOOKS BY LDP'S CEO, CA$H

TRUST IN NO MAN

TRUST IN NO MAN 2

TRUST IN NO MAN 3

BONDED BY BLOOD

SHORTY GOT A THUG

THUGS CRY

THUGS CRY 2

THUGS CRY 3

TRUST NO BITCH

TRUST NO BITCH 2

TRUST NO BITCH 3

TIL MY CASKET DROPS

RESTRAINING ORDER

RESTRAINING ORDER 2

IN LOVE WITH A CONVICT

LIFE OF A HOOD STAR

CPSIA information can be obtained
at www.ICGtesting.com
Printed in the USA
LVHW012334310821
696580LV00016B/1721